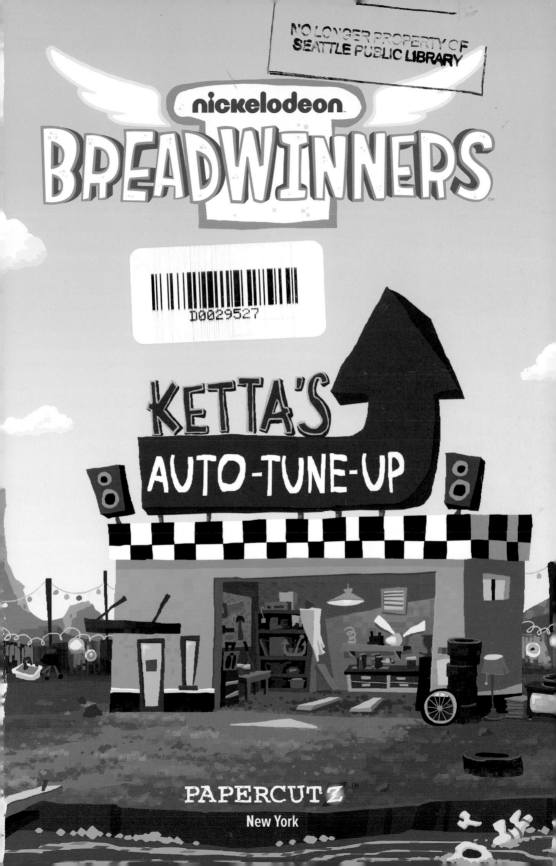

nickelodeon

BREADWINNERS™

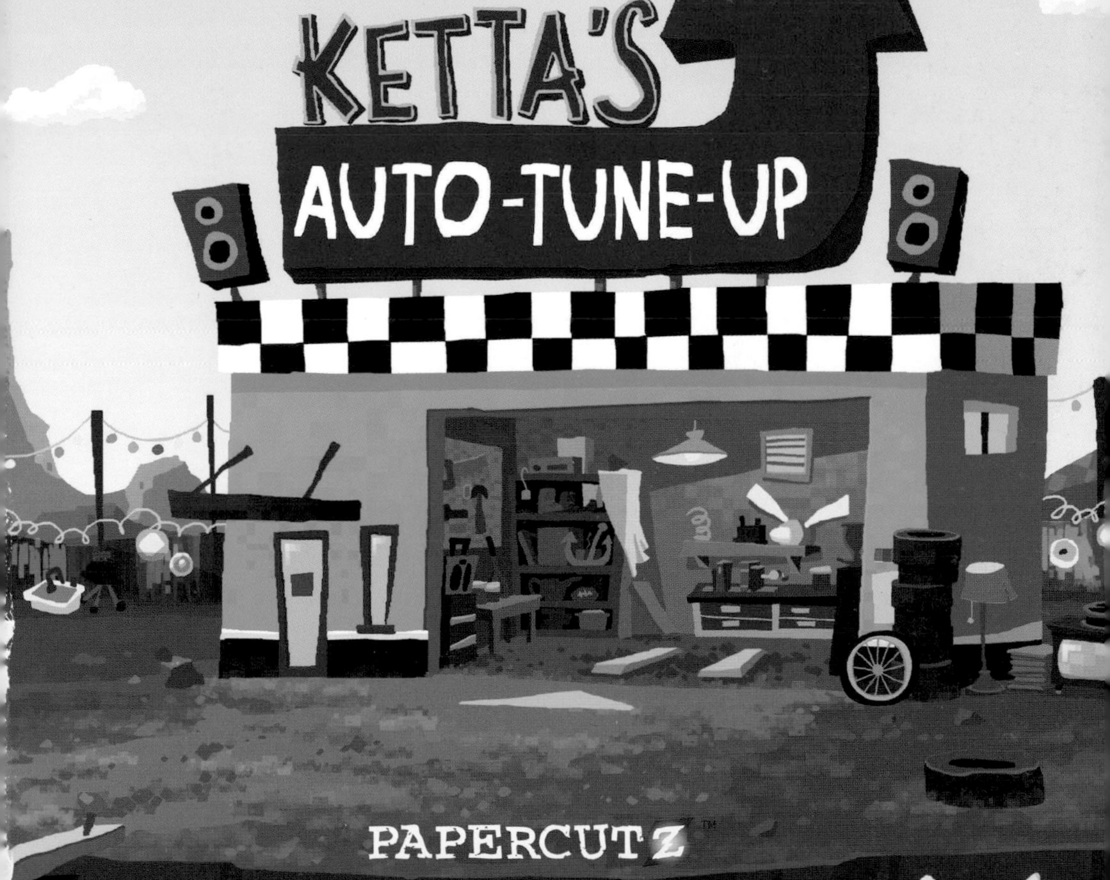
KETTA'S
AUTO-TUNE-UP

PAPERCUTZ™
New York

nickelodeon GRAPHIC NOVEL AVAILABLE FROM PAPERCUT

COMING SOON!

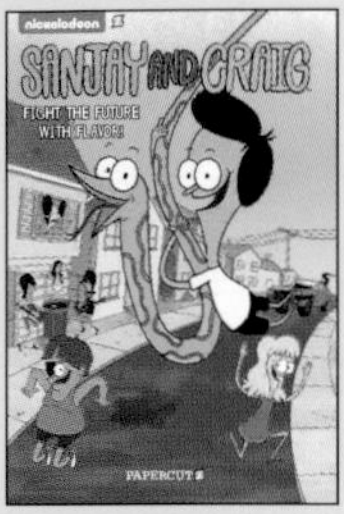
nickelodeon
SANJAY AND CRAIG
FIGHT THE FUTURE WITH FLAVOR!
PAPERCUTZ

#1 "Fight the Future with Flavor"

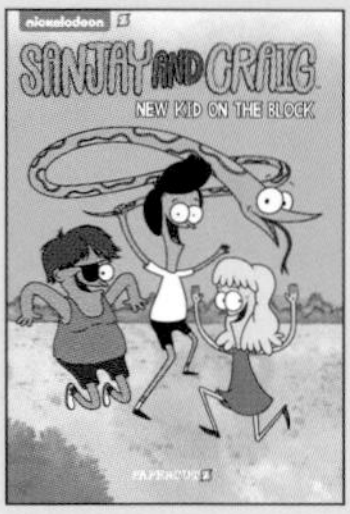
nickelodeon
SANJAY AND CRAIG
NEW KID ON THE BLOCK
PAPERCUTZ

#2 "New Kid on the Block"

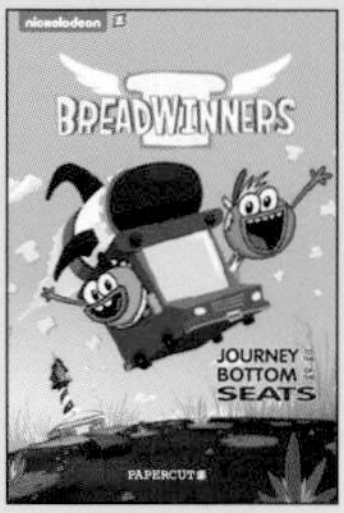
nickelodeon
BREADWINNERS
JOURNEY BOTTOM SEATS
PAPERCUTZ

#1 "Journey to the Bottom of the Seats"

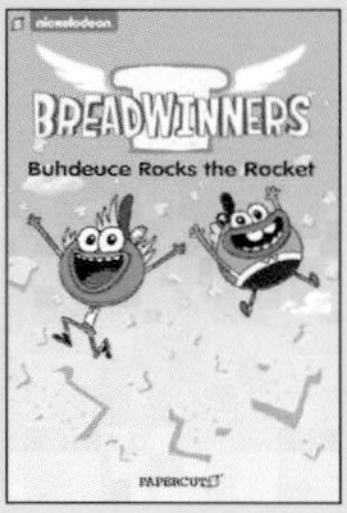
nickelodeon
BREADWINNERS
Buhdeuce Rocks the Rocket
PAPERCUTZ

#2 "Buhdeuce Rocks the Rocket"

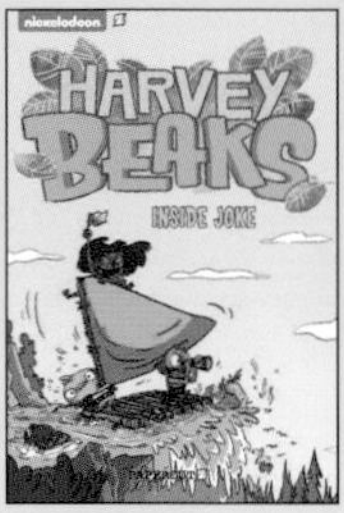
nickelodeon
HARVEY BEAKS
INSIDE JOKE

#1 "Inside Joke"

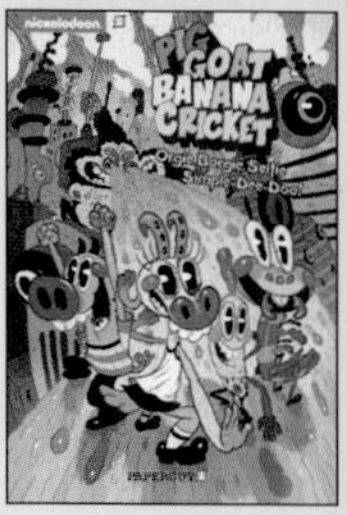
nickelodeon
PIG GOAT BANANA CRICKET
PAPERCUTZ

#1 "Orgle Borgle Selfie Simple-Dee-Doo!"

Nickelodeon graphic novels are available for $7.99 in paperback, $12.99 in hardcover. Available from booksellers everywhere. You can also order online from Papercutz.com, or call 1-800-886-1223, Monday through Friday, 9-5 EST. MC, Visa, and AmEx accepted. To order by mail, please add $4.00 for postage and handling for first book ordered, $1.00 for each additional book and make check payable to NBM Publishing.
Send to: Papercutz, 160 Broadway, Suite 700, East Wing, New York, NY 10038.

Nickelodeon graphic novels are also available digitally wherever e-books are sold.

SUBSCRIBE!

The Greatest Kids Magazine in the world is here and you can be a charter subscriber. Be the first to get your copies and make sure you don't miss a single issue of the all-new Nickelodeon Magazine!

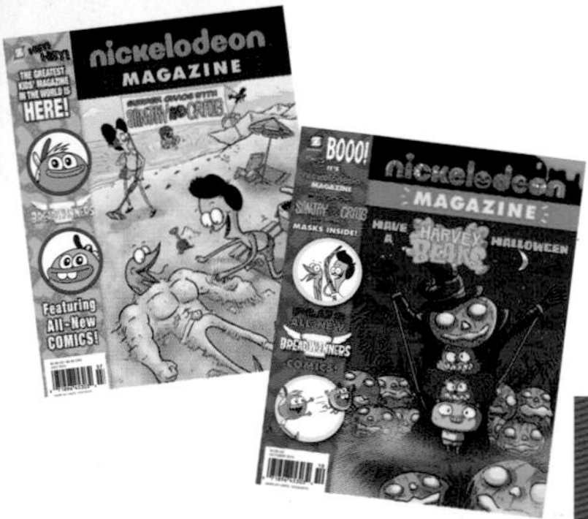
nickelodeon MAGAZINE
THE GREATEST KIDS' MAGAZINE IN THE WORLD IS HERE!
Featuring All-New COMICS!
BOOO!
nickelodeon MAGAZINE
MASKS INSIDE!
HAVE A HARVEY BEAKS HALLOWEEN

Never miss an issue of nickelodeon™ MAGAZINE

Get Your Copies Delivered Right to Your Mailbox at Home!

Save! And Get Free Issues!

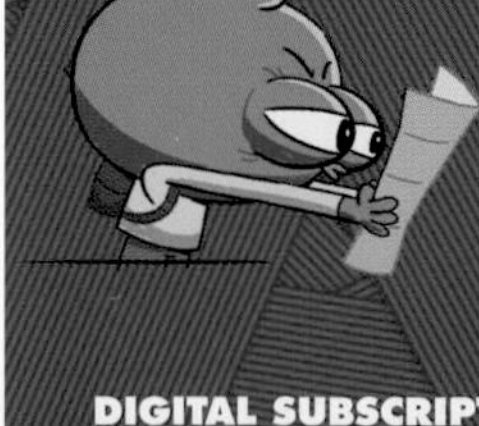

7 ISSUES FOR THE PRICE OF 6!

+SAVE $7 OFF COVER PRICE!

6 REGULAR ISSUES
+1 BONUS FREE ISSUE
7 ISSUES FOR ONLY $27.50

14 ISSUES FOR THE PRICE OF 12!

+SAVE $14 OFF COVER PRICE!

12 REGULAR ISSUES
+2 BONUS FREE ISSUES
14 ISSUES FOR ONLY $49.99

DIGITAL SUBSCRIPTION - ONLY $19.99 - OR FREE FOR ALL PRINT SUBSCRIBERS!

ORDER ONLINE at Papercutz.com/nickmag

OR CALL 1-800-778-6278

(Please have debit/credit card ready)

Use promo code: BWGN2.

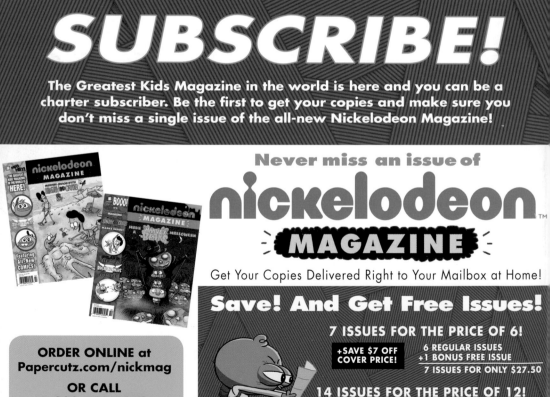

TABLE OF CONTENTS

Buhdeuce Rocks the Rocket 5

Spaghetti Getaway 16

Gingerbread Sam 23

Jellymilk ... Amok! 41

#2 Buhdeuce Rocks the Rocket

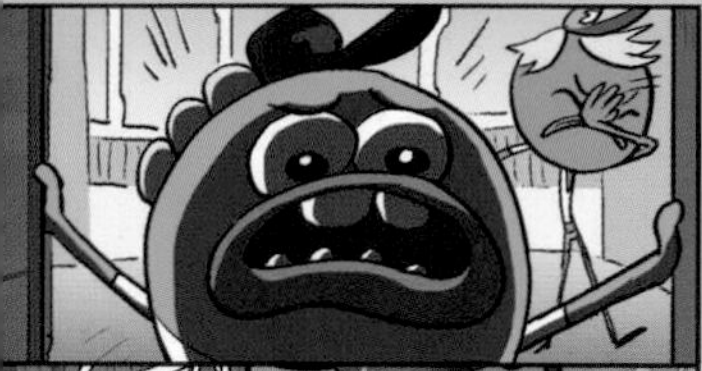

"BUHDEUCE ROCKS THE ROCKET"
Stefan Petrucha – Writer
Allison Strejlau – Artist
Tom Orzechowski – Letterer
Laurie E. Smith – Colorist

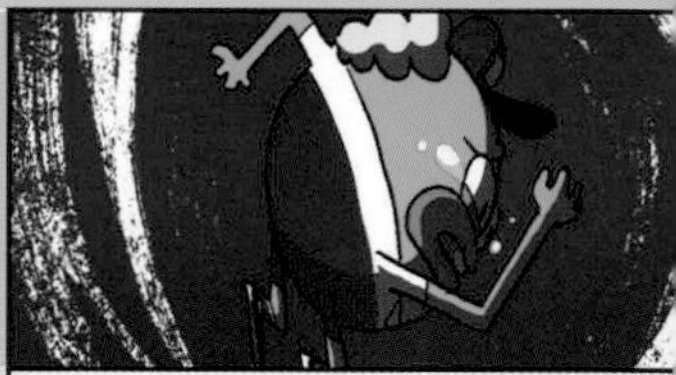

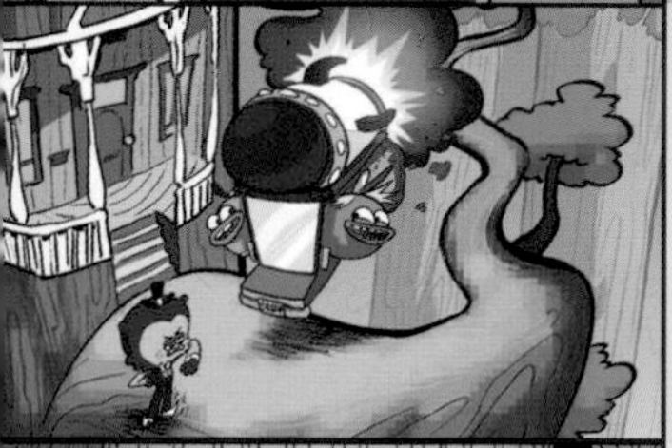

"SPAGHETTI GETAWAY"
Stefan Petrucha – Writer
Based on an idea by The Breadwinners Show Writers
Allison Strejlau – Artist
Tom Orzechowski – Letterer
Matt Herms – Colorist

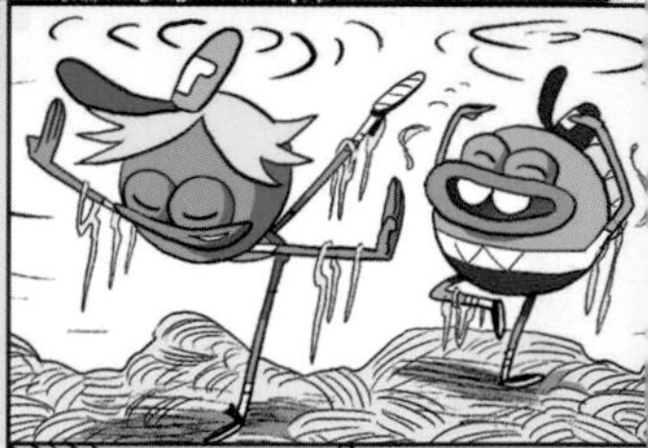

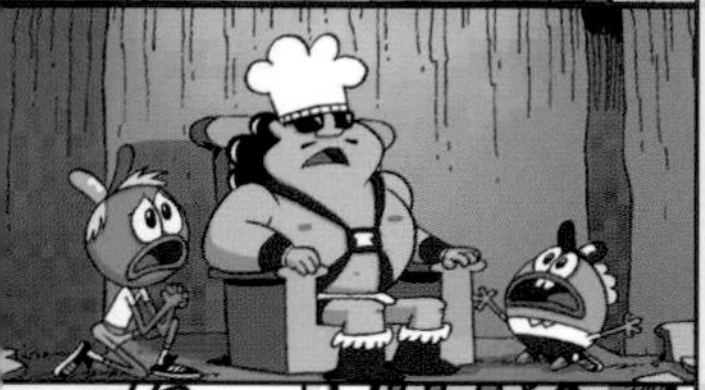

"GINGERBREAD SAM"
Stefan Petrucha – Writer
Mike Kazaleh – Artist
Tom Orzechowski – Letterer
Matteo Baldrighi – Colorist

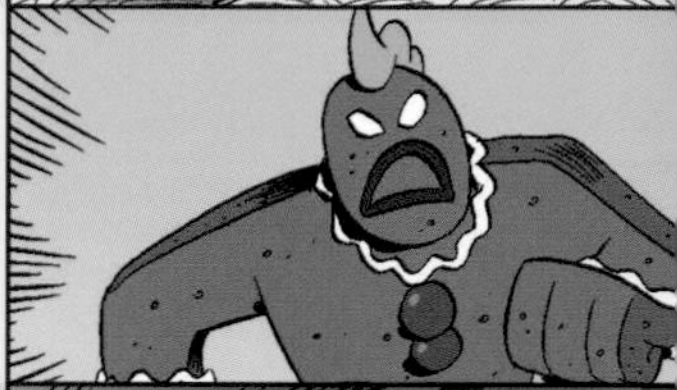

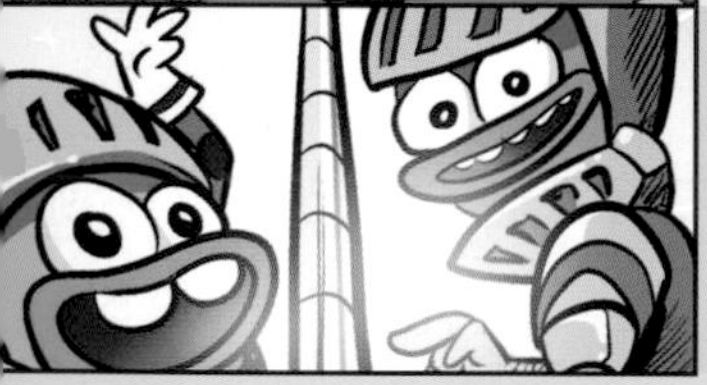

"JELLYMILK ... AMOK!"
Stefan Petrucha – Writer
Allison Strejlau – Artist
Janice Chiang – Letterer
Matt Herms – Colorist

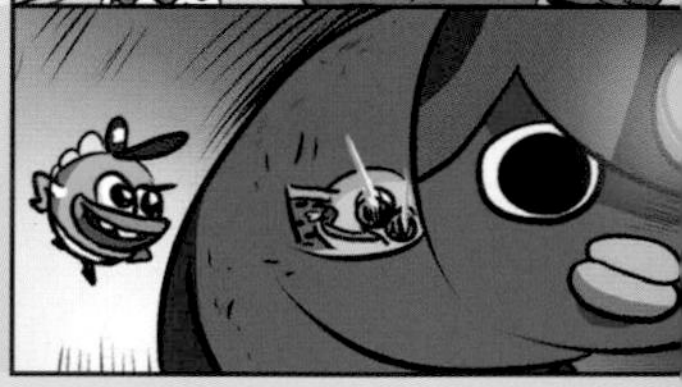

Based on the Nickelodeon animated TV series
created by Gary "Doodles" DiRaffaele and Steve Borst

James Salerno – Sr. Art Director/Nickelodeon
Chris Nelson – Design/Production
Jeff Whitman – Production Coordinator
Bethany Bryan – Editor
Joan Hilty – Comics Editor/Nickelodeon
Asante Simons – Editorial Intern
Jim Salicrup
Editor-in-Chief

ISBN: 978-1-62991-437-4 paperback edition
ISBN: 978-1-62991-438-1 hardcover edition

Papercutz books may be purchased for business or promotional use. For information on bulk purchases please contact Macmillan Corporate and Premium Sales Department at (800) 221-7945 x5442.

Printed in China
March 2016 by O.G. Printing Productions, LTD.
26/Fl, 625 King's Road
North Point, Hong Kong
China

Distributed by Macmillan
First Printing

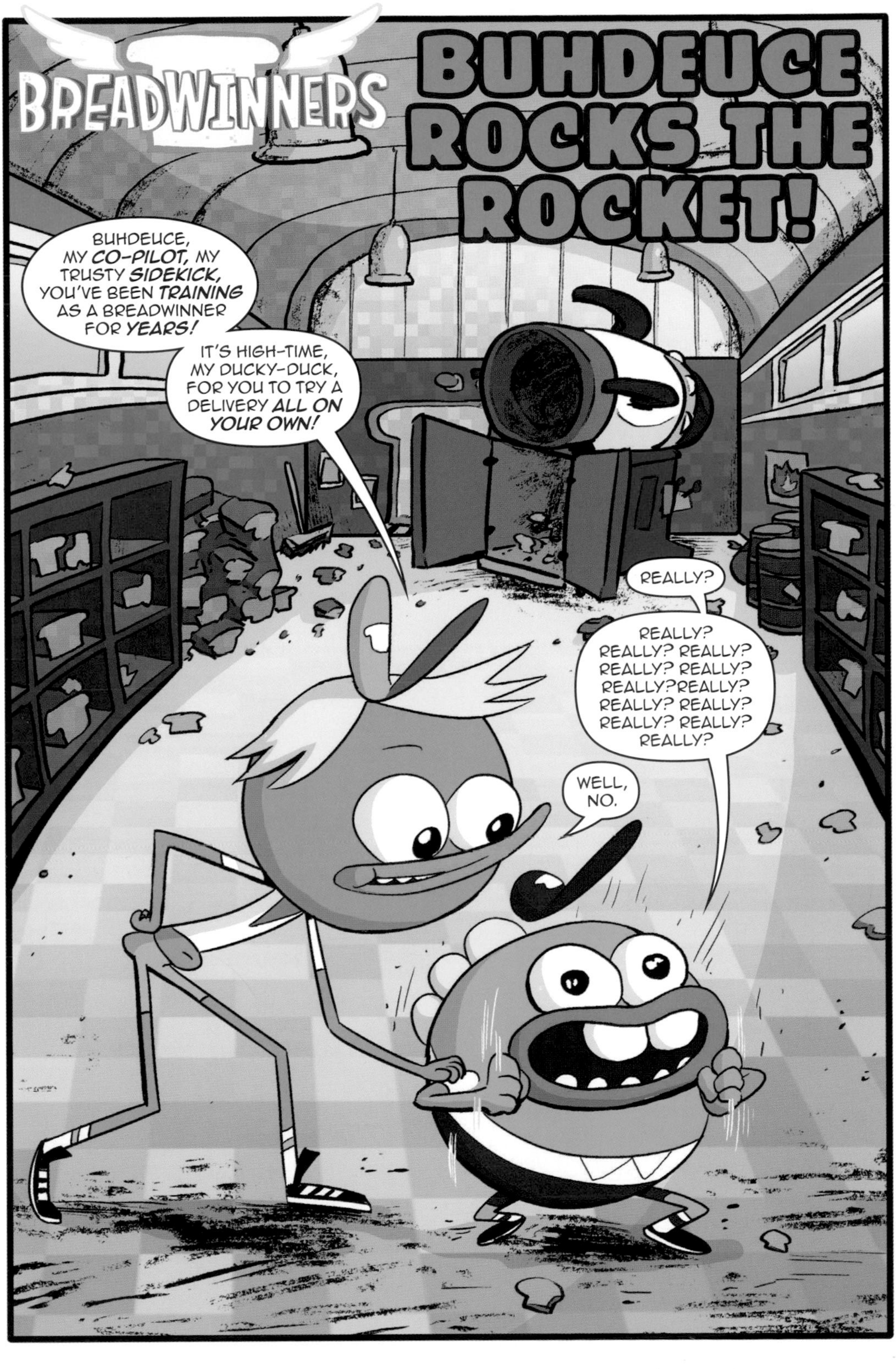
BREADWINNERS
BUHDEUCE ROCKS THE ROCKET!
BUHDEUCE, MY CO-PILOT, MY TRUSTY SIDEKICK, YOU'VE BEEN TRAINING AS A BREADWINNER FOR YEARS!
IT'S HIGH-TIME, MY DUCKY-DUCK, FOR YOU TO TRY A DELIVERY ALL ON YOUR OWN!
REALLY?
REALLY? REALLY? REALLY? REALLY? REALLY? REALLY?REALLY? REALLY? REALLY? REALLY? REALLY? REALLY?
WELL, NO.

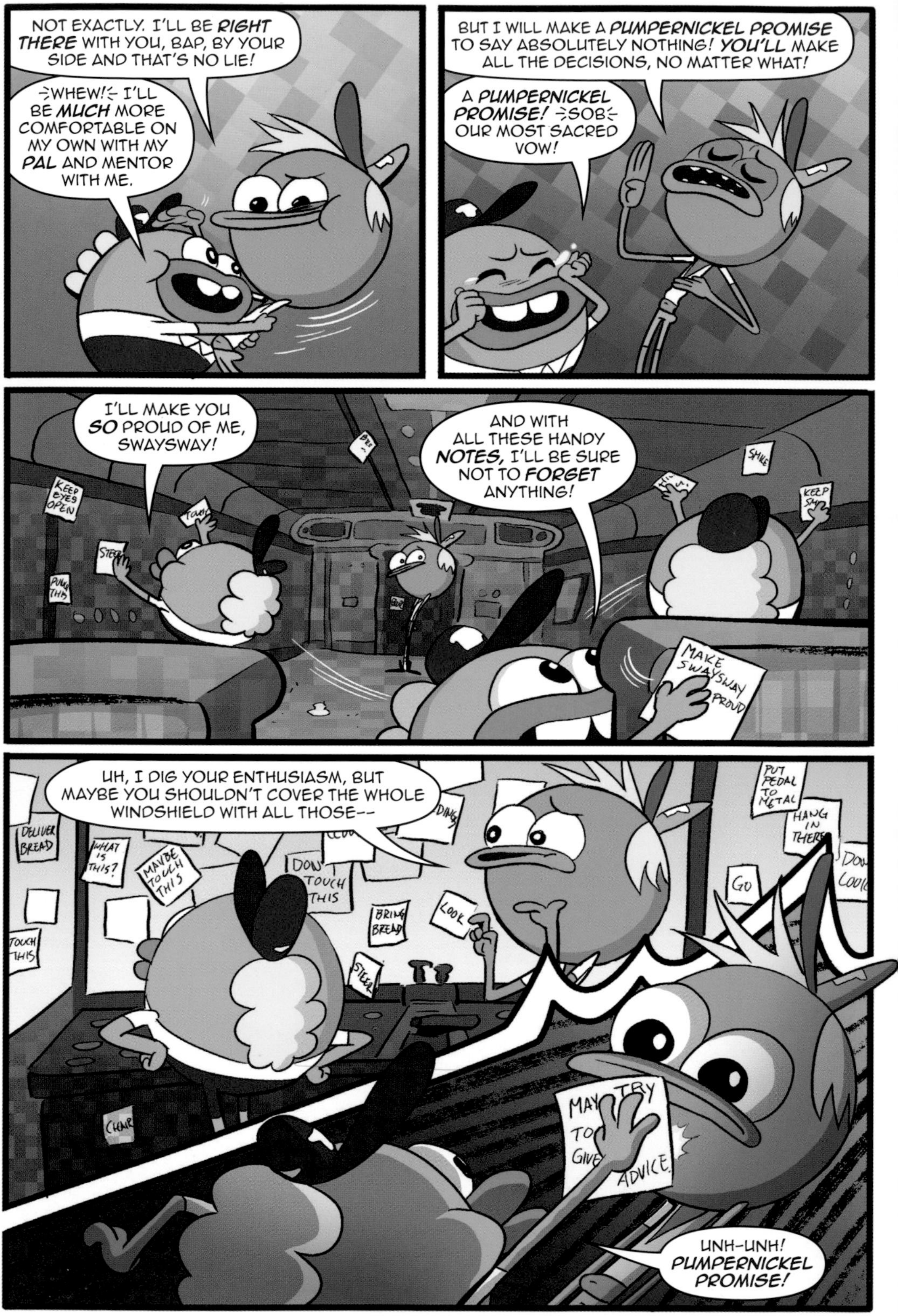
NOT EXACTLY. I'LL BE RIGHT THERE WITH YOU, BAP, BY YOUR SIDE AND THAT'S NO LIE!
WHEW! I'LL BE MUCH MORE COMFORTABLE ON MY OWN WITH MY PAL AND MENTOR WITH ME.
BUT I WILL MAKE A PUMPERNICKEL PROMISE TO SAY ABSOLUTELY NOTHING! YOU'LL MAKE ALL THE DECISIONS, NO MATTER WHAT!
A PUMPERNICKEL PROMISE! SOB OUR MOST SACRED VOW!
I'LL MAKE YOU SO PROUD OF ME, SWAYSWAY!
KEEP EYES OPEN
AND WITH ALL THESE HANDY NOTES, I'LL BE SURE NOT TO FORGET ANYTHING!
MAKE SWAYSWAY PROUD
UH, I DIG YOUR ENTHUSIASM, BUT MAYBE YOU SHOULDN'T COVER THE WHOLE WINDSHIELD WITH ALL THOSE--
DELIVER BREAD
WHAT IS THIS?
MAYBE TOUCH THIS
DON'T TOUCH THIS
BRING BREAD
LOOK
PUT PEDAL TO METAL
GO
CHAIR
UNH-UNH! PUMPERNICKEL PROMISE!

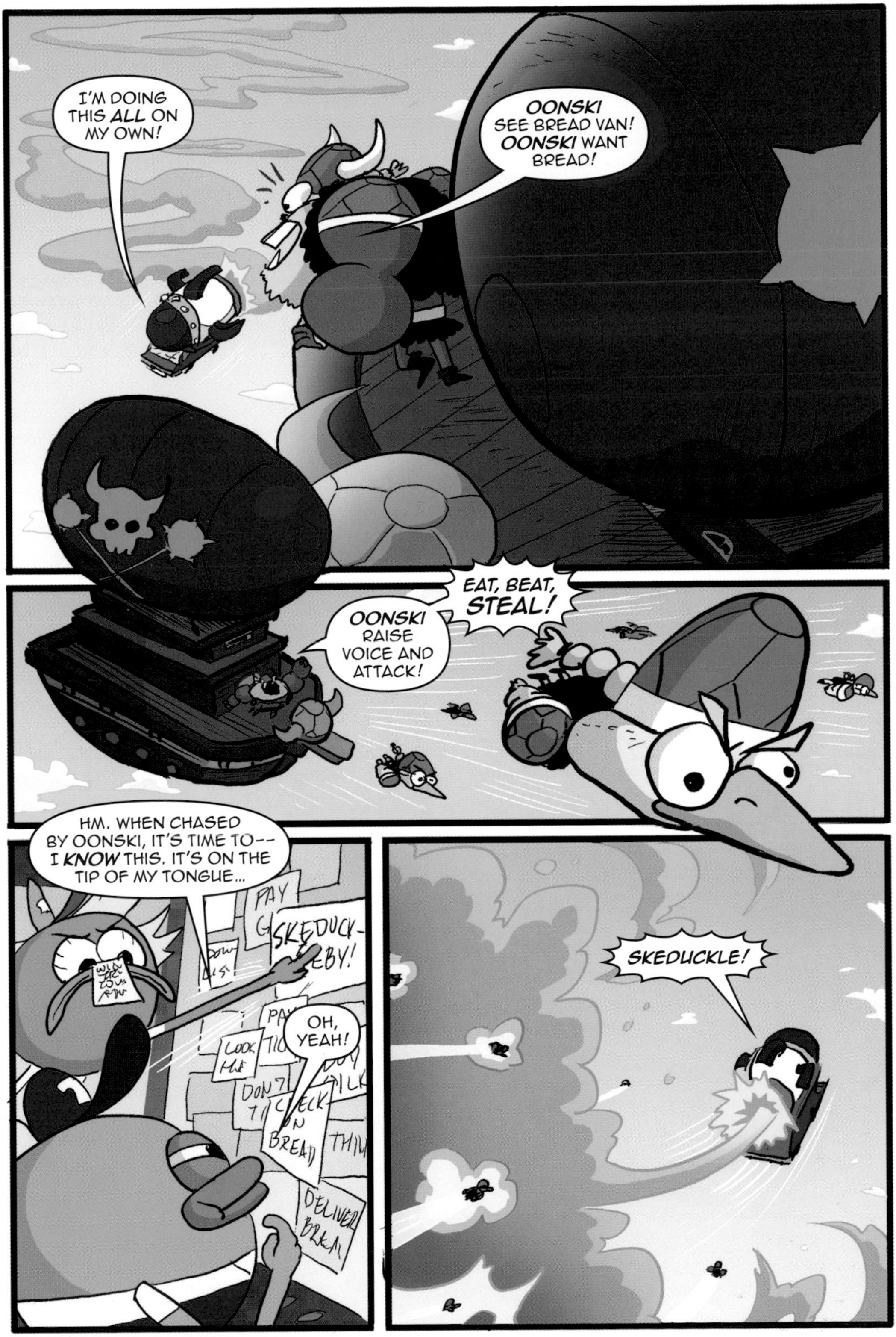
I'M DOING THIS ALL ON MY OWN!
OONSKI SEE BREAD VAN! OONSKI WANT BREAD!
OONSKI RAISE VOICE AND ATTACK!
EAT, BEAT, STEAL!
HM. WHEN CHASED BY OONSKI, IT'S TIME TO-- I KNOW THIS. IT'S ON THE TIP OF MY TONGUE...
OH, YEAH!
SKEDUCKLE!

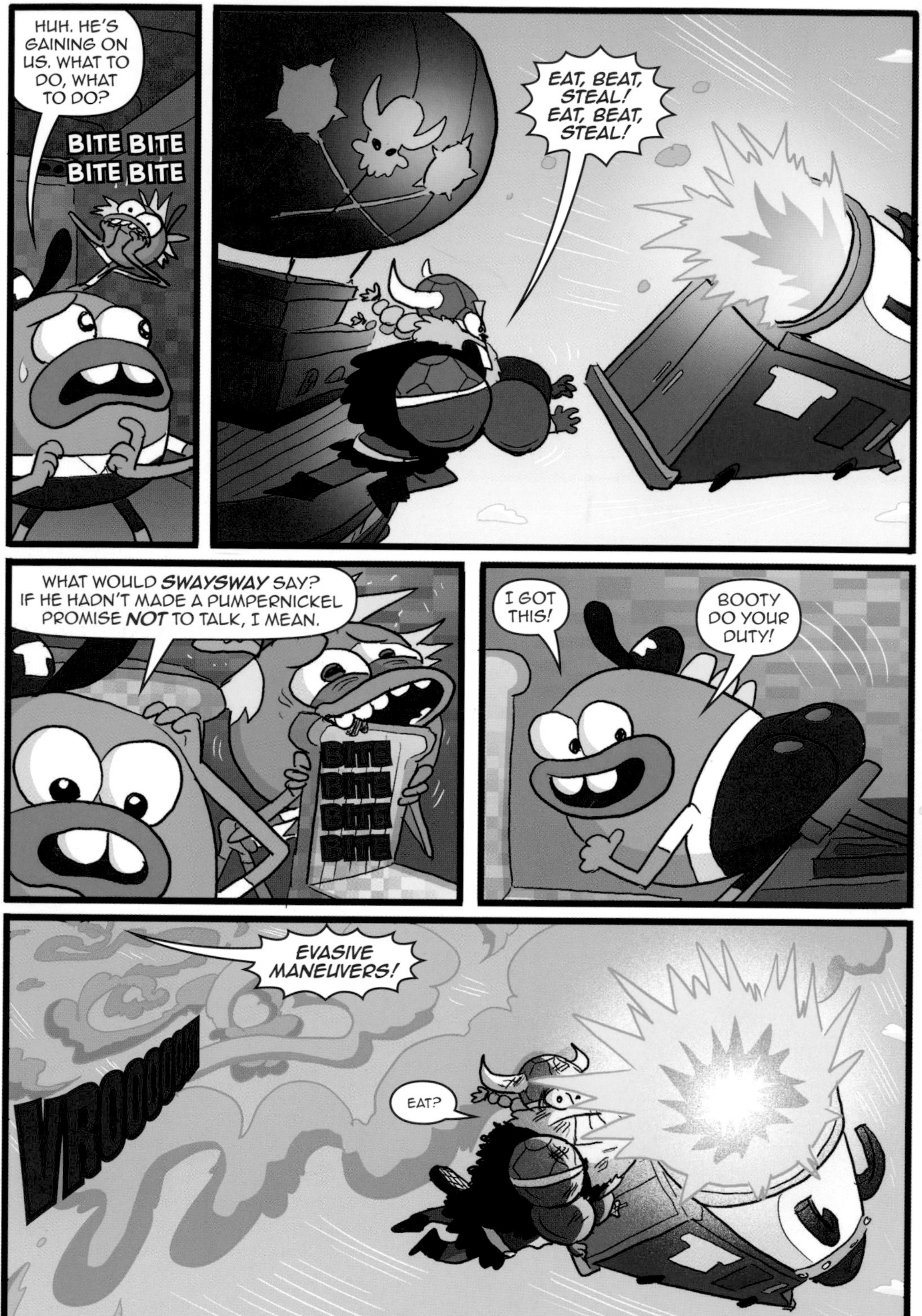
HUH. HE'S GAINING ON US. WHAT TO DO, WHAT TO DO?
BITE BITE BITE BITE
EAT, BEAT, STEAL! EAT, BEAT, STEAL!
WHAT WOULD SWAYSWAY SAY? IF HE HADN'T MADE A PUMPERNICKEL PROMISE NOT TO TALK, I MEAN.
BITE BITE BITE BITE
I GOT THIS!
BOOTY DO YOUR DUTY!
EVASIVE MANEUVERS!
VROOOOM
EAT?

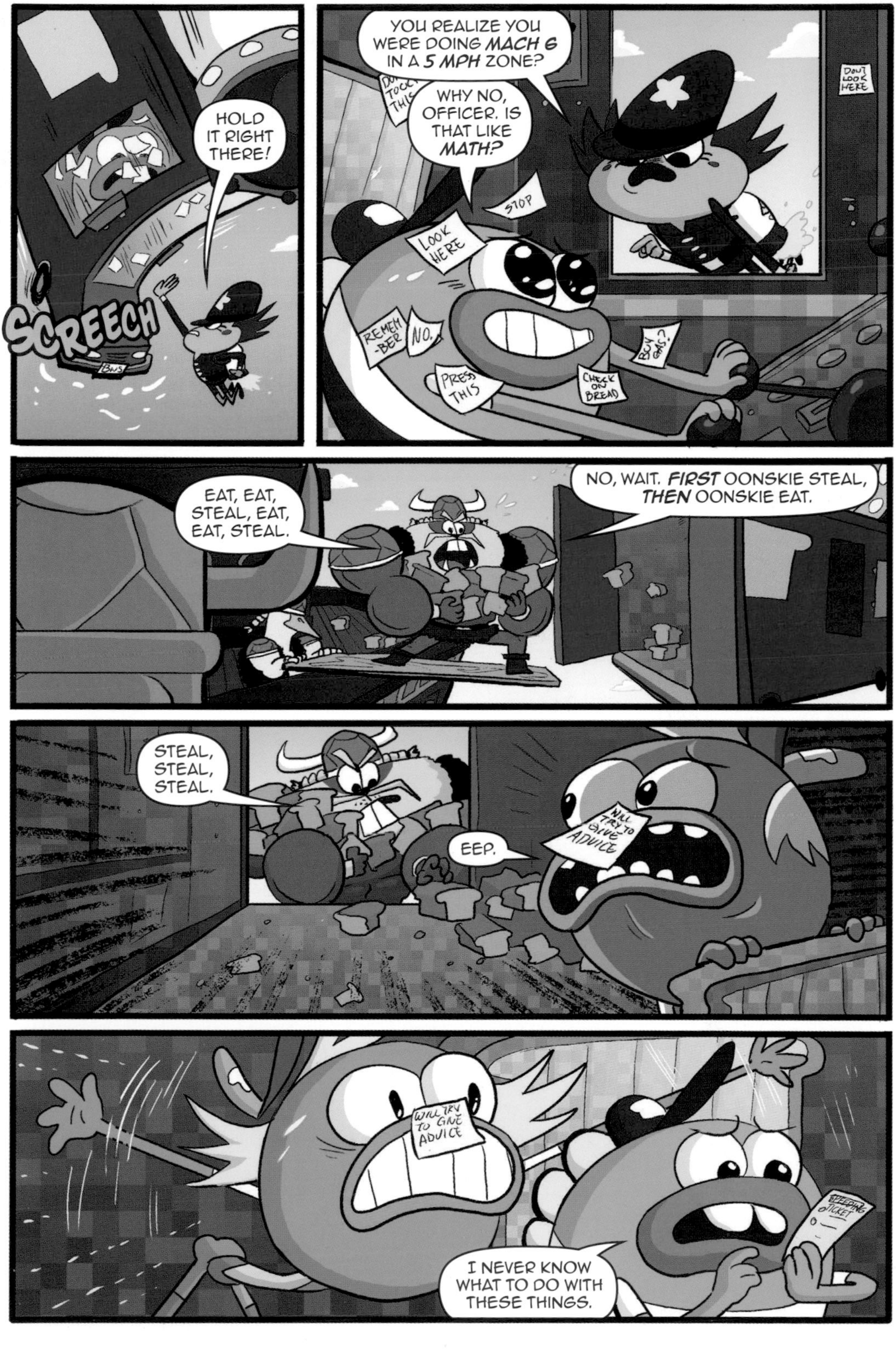
HOLD IT RIGHT THERE!
SCREECH
BUS
YOU REALIZE YOU WERE DOING MACH 6 IN A 5 MPH ZONE?
WHY NO, OFFICER. IS THAT LIKE MATH?
DON'T LOOK HERE
STOP
LOOK HERE
REMEM-BER
NO.
PRESS THIS
CHECK ON BREAD
BUY GAS?
EAT, EAT, STEAL, EAT, EAT, STEAL.
NO, WAIT. FIRST OONSKIE STEAL, THEN OONSKIE EAT.
STEAL, STEAL, STEAL.
EEP.
WILL TRY TO GIVE ADVICE
WILL TRY TO GIVE ADVICE
SPEEDING TICKET
I NEVER KNOW WHAT TO DO WITH THESE THINGS.

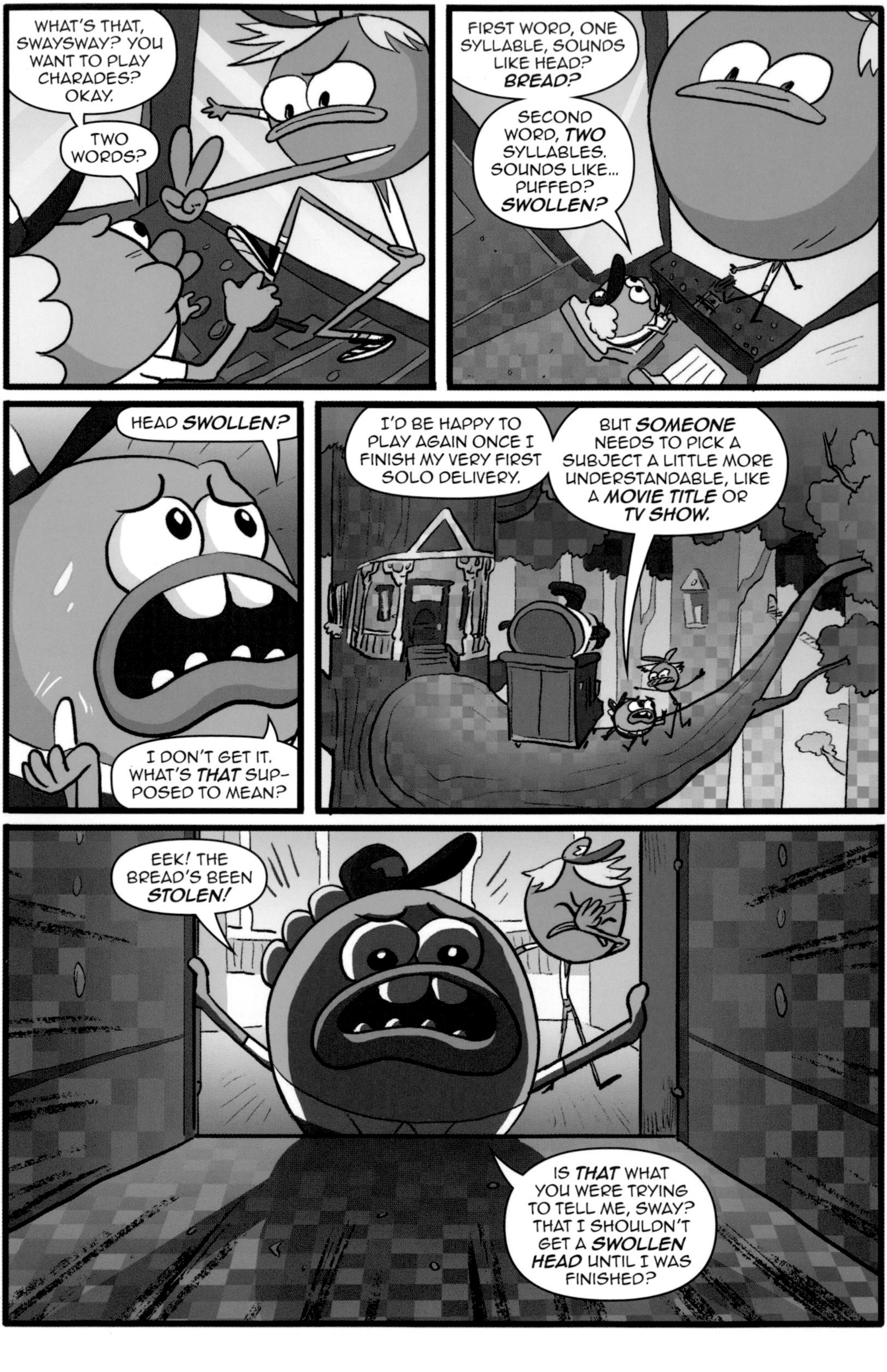
WHAT'S THAT, SWAYSWAY? YOU WANT TO PLAY CHARADES? OKAY.
TWO WORDS?
FIRST WORD, ONE SYLLABLE, SOUNDS LIKE HEAD? *BREAD?*
SECOND WORD, *TWO* SYLLABLES. SOUNDS LIKE... PUFFED? *SWOLLEN?*
HEAD *SWOLLEN?*
I DON'T GET IT. WHAT'S *THAT* SUP-POSED TO MEAN?
I'D BE HAPPY TO PLAY AGAIN ONCE I FINISH MY VERY FIRST SOLO DELIVERY.
BUT *SOMEONE* NEEDS TO PICK A SUBJECT A LITTLE MORE UNDERSTANDABLE, LIKE A *MOVIE TITLE* OR *TV SHOW.*
EEK! THE BREAD'S BEEN *STOLEN!*
IS *THAT* WHAT YOU WERE TRYING TO TELL ME, SWAY? THAT I SHOULDN'T GET A *SWOLLEN HEAD* UNTIL I WAS FINISHED?

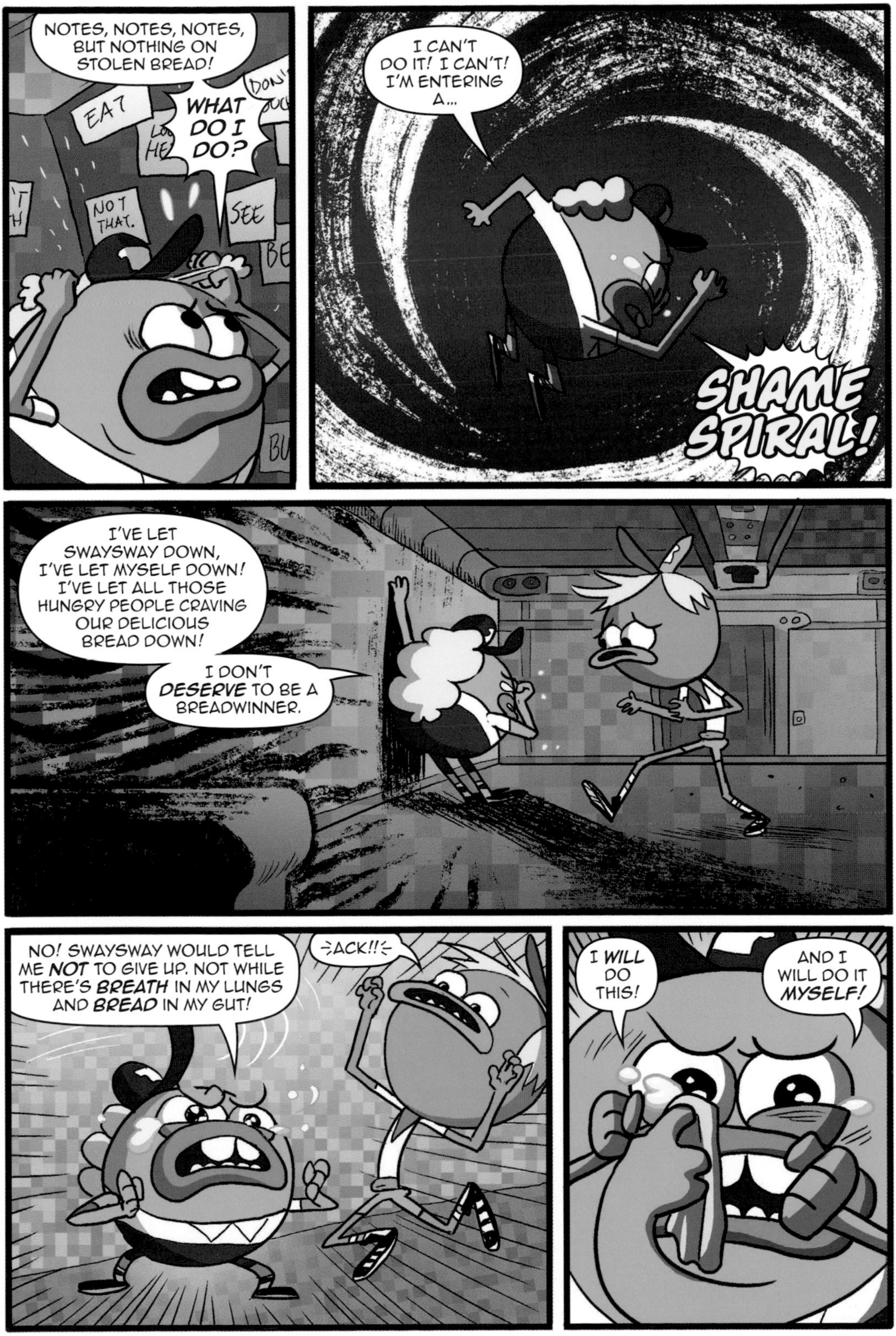

NOTES, NOTES, NOTES, BUT NOTHING ON STOLEN BREAD!
WHAT DO I DO?
EAT
NOT THAT.
SEE
I CAN'T DO IT! I CAN'T! I'M ENTERING A...
SHAME SPIRAL!
I'VE LET SWAYSWAY DOWN, I'VE LET MYSELF DOWN! I'VE LET ALL THOSE HUNGRY PEOPLE CRAVING OUR DELICIOUS BREAD DOWN!
I DON'T DESERVE TO BE A BREADWINNER.
NO! SWAYSWAY WOULD TELL ME NOT TO GIVE UP. NOT WHILE THERE'S BREATH IN MY LUNGS AND BREAD IN MY GUT!
ACK!!
I WILL DO THIS!
AND I WILL DO IT MYSELF!

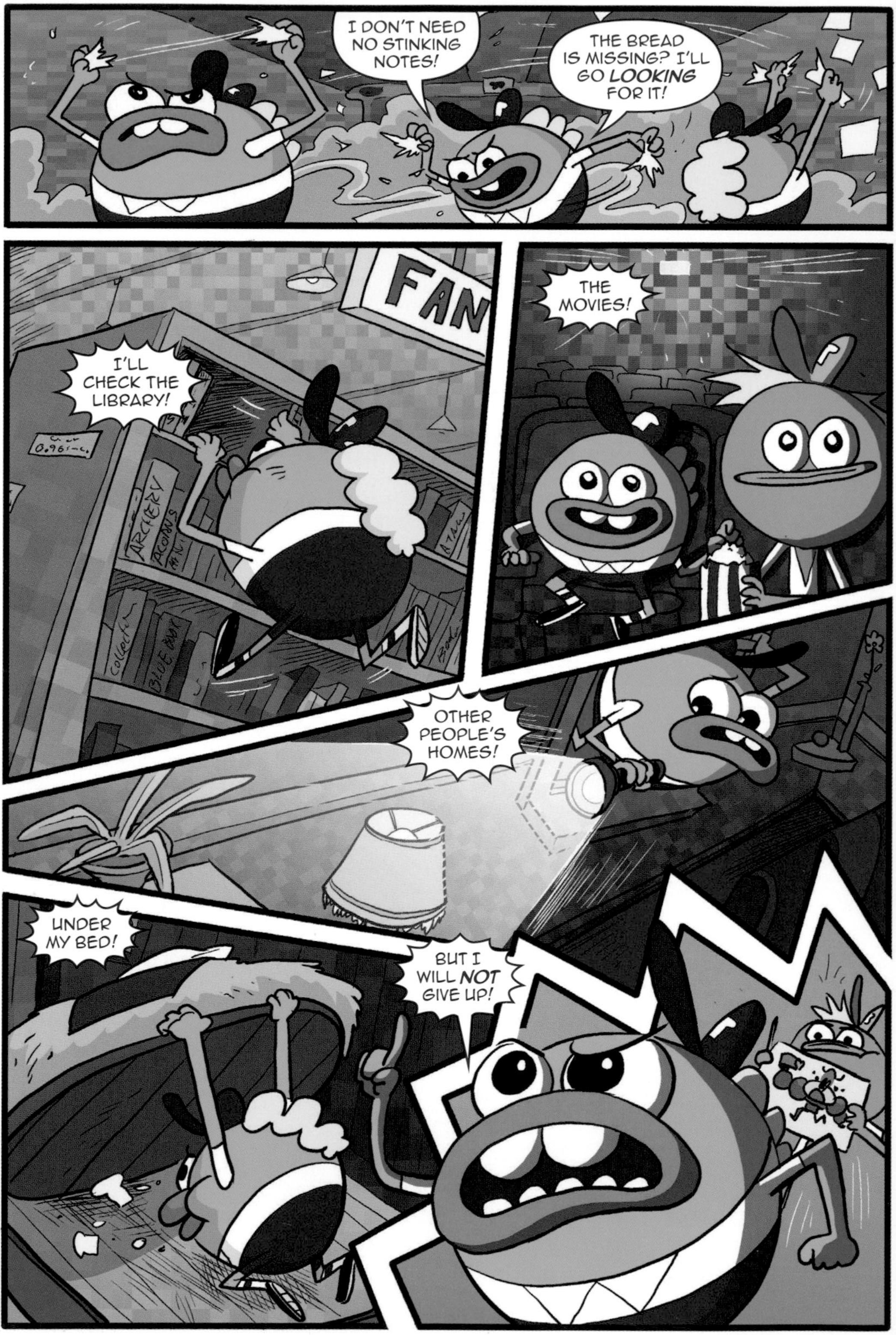
I DON'T NEED NO STINKING NOTES!
THE BREAD IS MISSING? I'LL GO **LOOKING** FOR IT!
FAN
I'LL CHECK THE LIBRARY!
THE MOVIES!
OTHER PEOPLE'S HOMES!
UNDER MY BED!
BUT I WILL **NOT** GIVE UP!

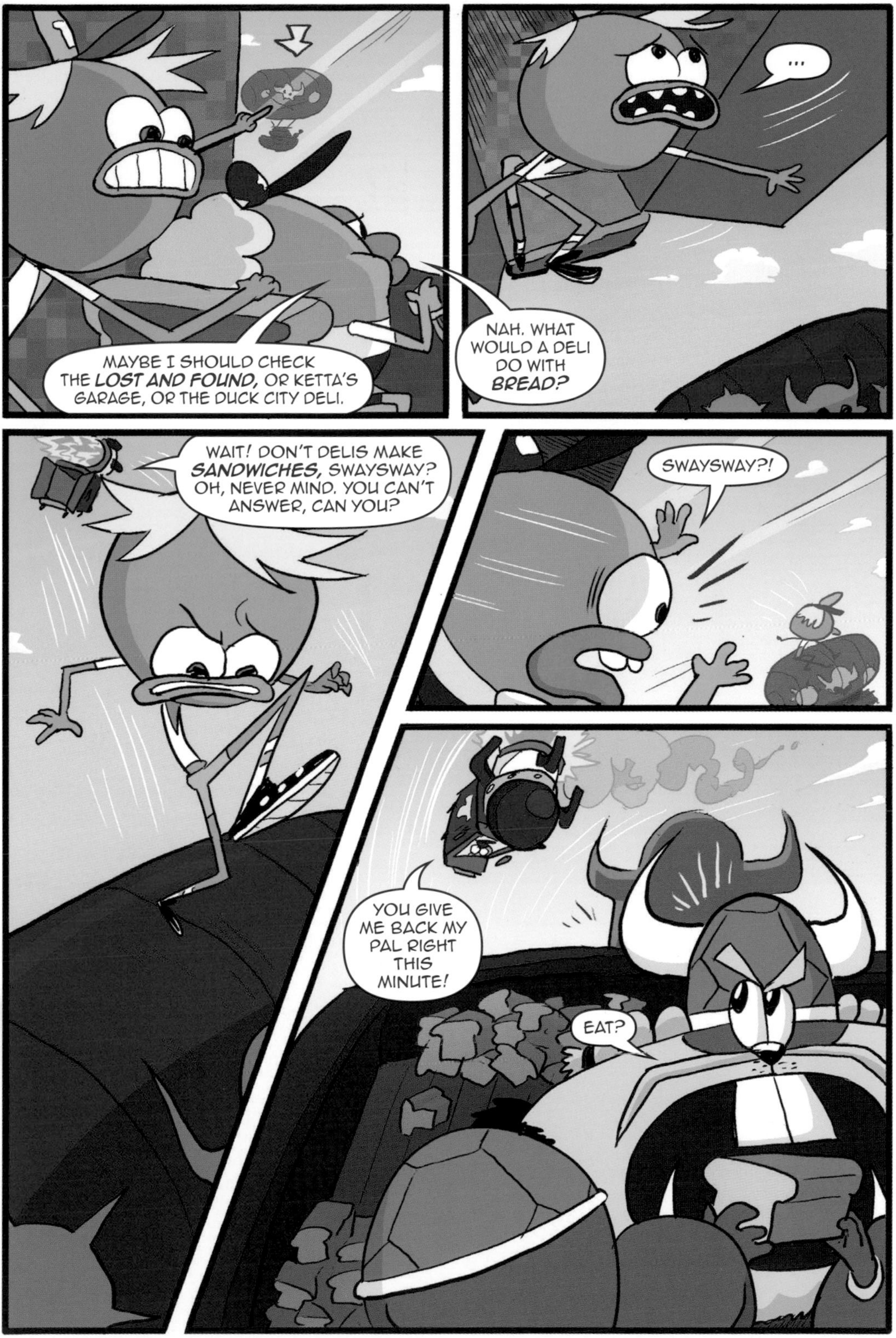
MAYBE I SHOULD CHECK THE **LOST AND FOUND,** OR KETTA'S GARAGE, OR THE DUCK CITY DELI.
NAH. WHAT WOULD A DELI DO WITH **BREAD?**
...
WAIT! DON'T DELIS MAKE **SANDWICHES,** SWAYSWAY? OH, NEVER MIND. YOU CAN'T ANSWER, CAN YOU?
SWAYSWAY?!
YOU GIVE ME BACK MY PAL RIGHT THIS MINUTE!
EAT?

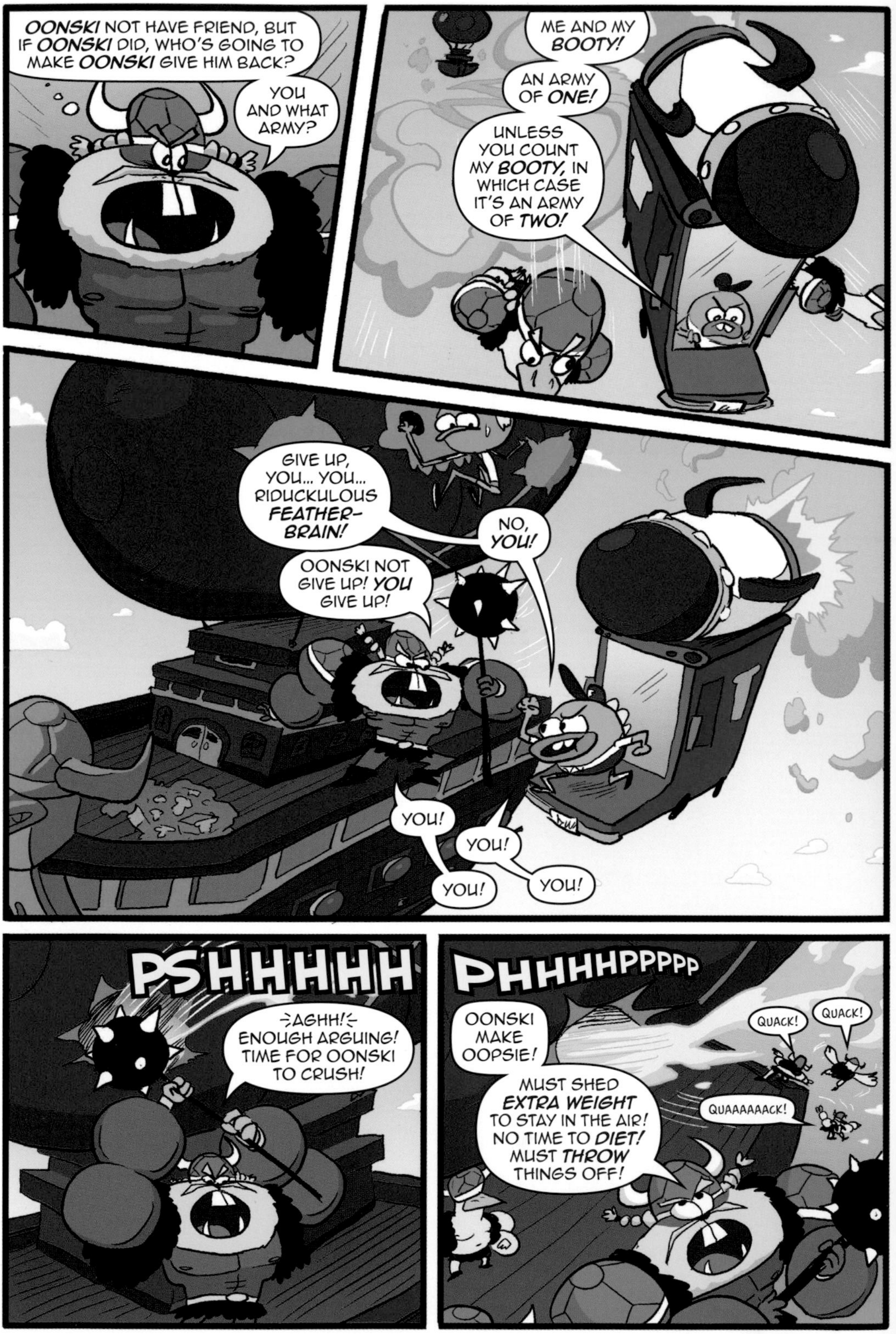

OONSKI NOT HAVE FRIEND, BUT IF OONSKI DID, WHO'S GOING TO MAKE OONSKI GIVE HIM BACK?
YOU AND WHAT ARMY?
ME AND MY BOOTY!
AN ARMY OF ONE!
UNLESS YOU COUNT MY BOOTY, IN WHICH CASE IT'S AN ARMY OF TWO!
GIVE UP, YOU... YOU... RIDUCKULOUS FEATHER-BRAIN!
NO, YOU!
OONSKI NOT GIVE UP! YOU GIVE UP!
YOU!
YOU!
YOU!
YOU!
PSHHHHHH
AGHH!
ENOUGH ARGUING! TIME FOR OONSKI TO CRUSH!
PHHHHPPPPP
OONSKI MAKE OOPSIE!
MUST SHED EXTRA WEIGHT TO STAY IN THE AIR! NO TIME TO DIET! MUST THROW THINGS OFF!
QUACK!
QUACK!
QUAAAAAACK!

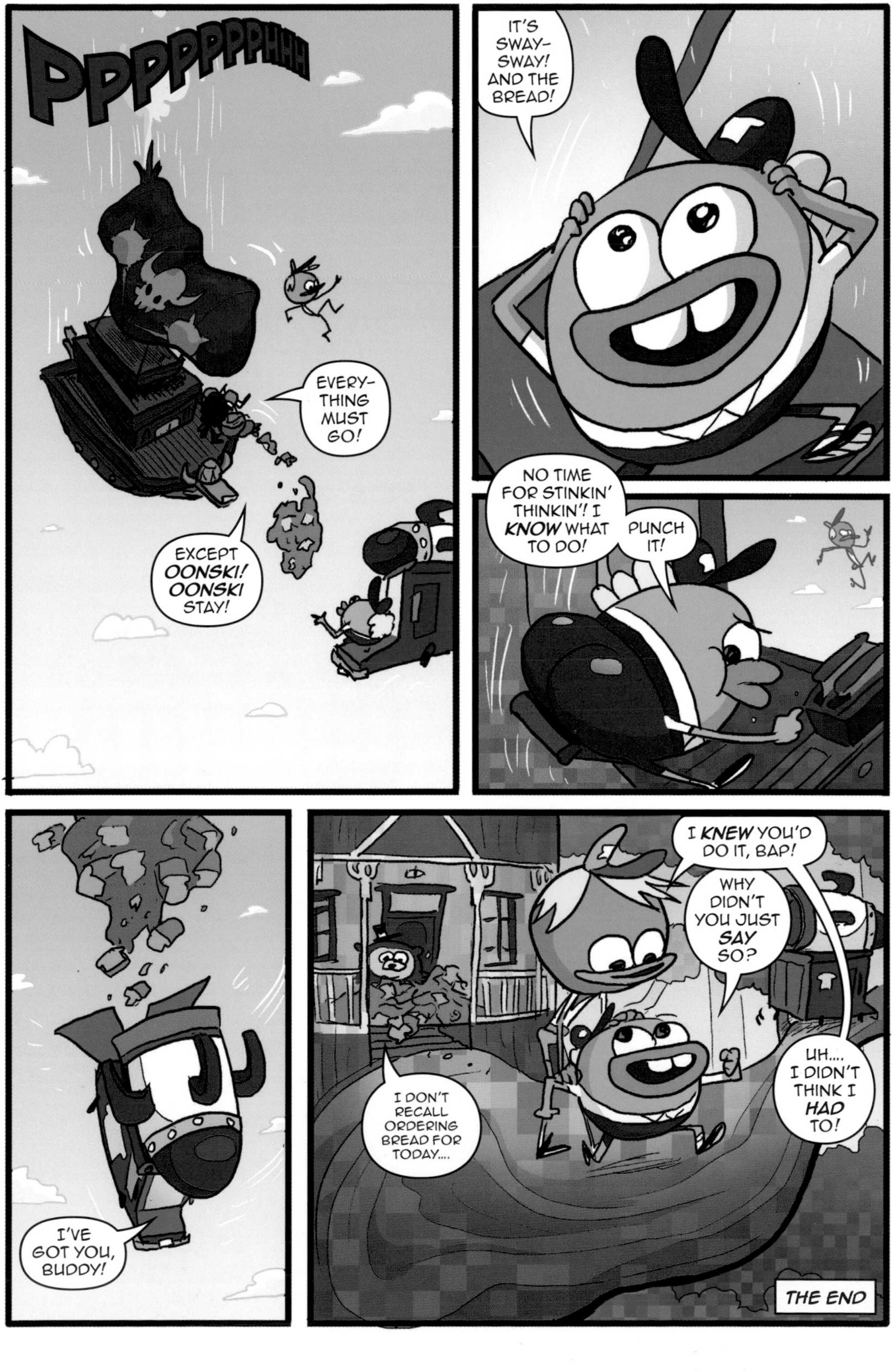
PPPPPPPHHH
EVERY-THING MUST GO!
EXCEPT OONSKI! OONSKI STAY!
IT'S SWAY-SWAY! AND THE BREAD!
NO TIME FOR STINKIN' THINKIN'! I **KNOW** WHAT TO DO!
PUNCH IT!
I'VE GOT YOU, BUDDY!
I **KNEW** YOU'D DO IT, BAP!
WHY DIDN'T YOU JUST **SAY** SO?
I DON'T RECALL ORDERING BREAD FOR TODAY....
UH.... I DIDN'T THINK I **HAD** TO!
THE END

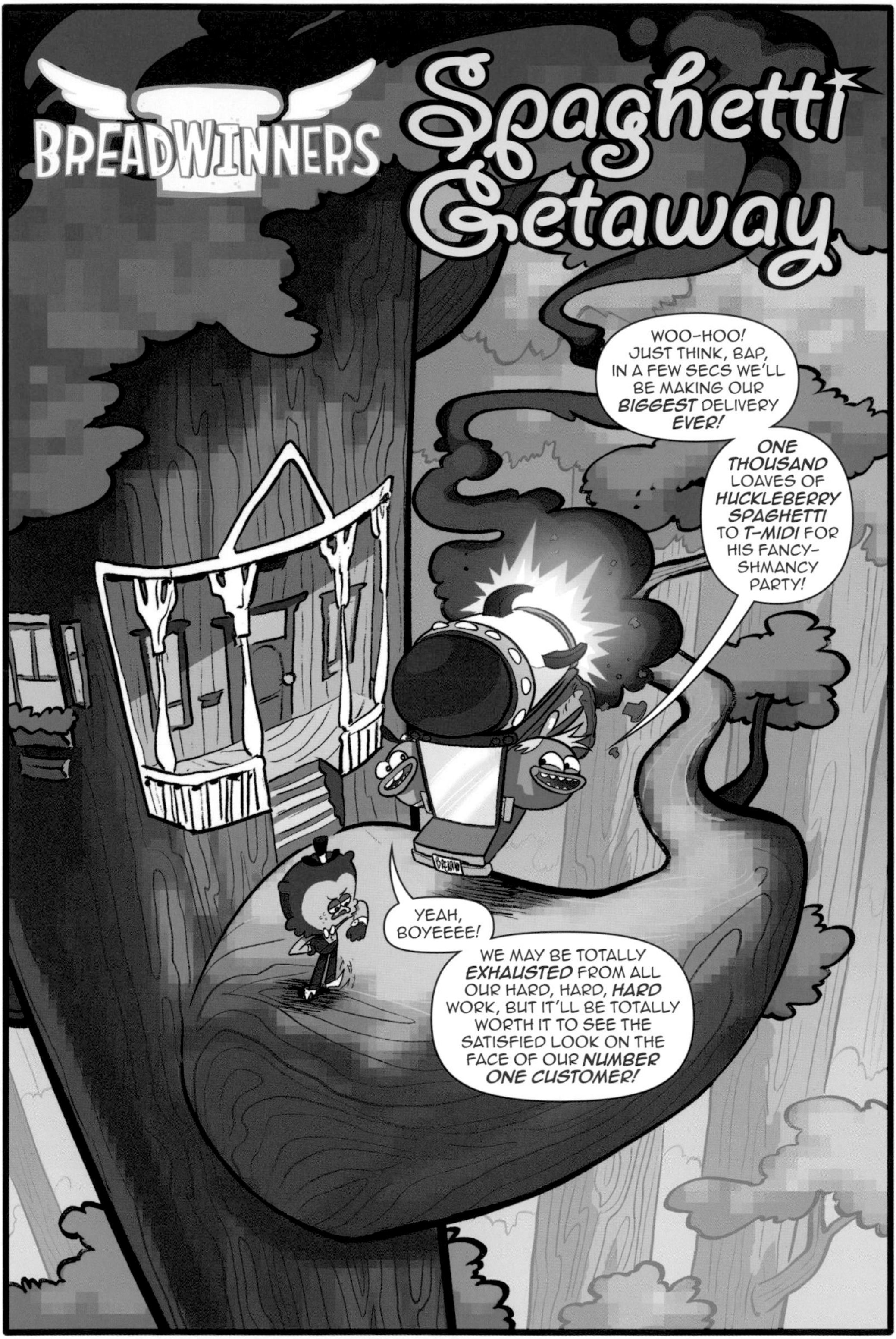
BREADWINNERS
Spaghetti Getaway
WOO-HOO! JUST THINK, BAP, IN A FEW SECS WE'LL BE MAKING OUR BIGGEST DELIVERY EVER!
ONE THOUSAND LOAVES OF HUCKLEBERRY SPAGHETTI TO T-MIDI FOR HIS FANCY-SHMANCY PARTY!
YEAH, BOYEEEE!
WE MAY BE TOTALLY EXHAUSTED FROM ALL OUR HARD, HARD, HARD WORK, BUT IT'LL BE TOTALLY WORTH IT TO SEE THE SATISFIED LOOK ON THE FACE OF OUR NUMBER ONE CUSTOMER!

17

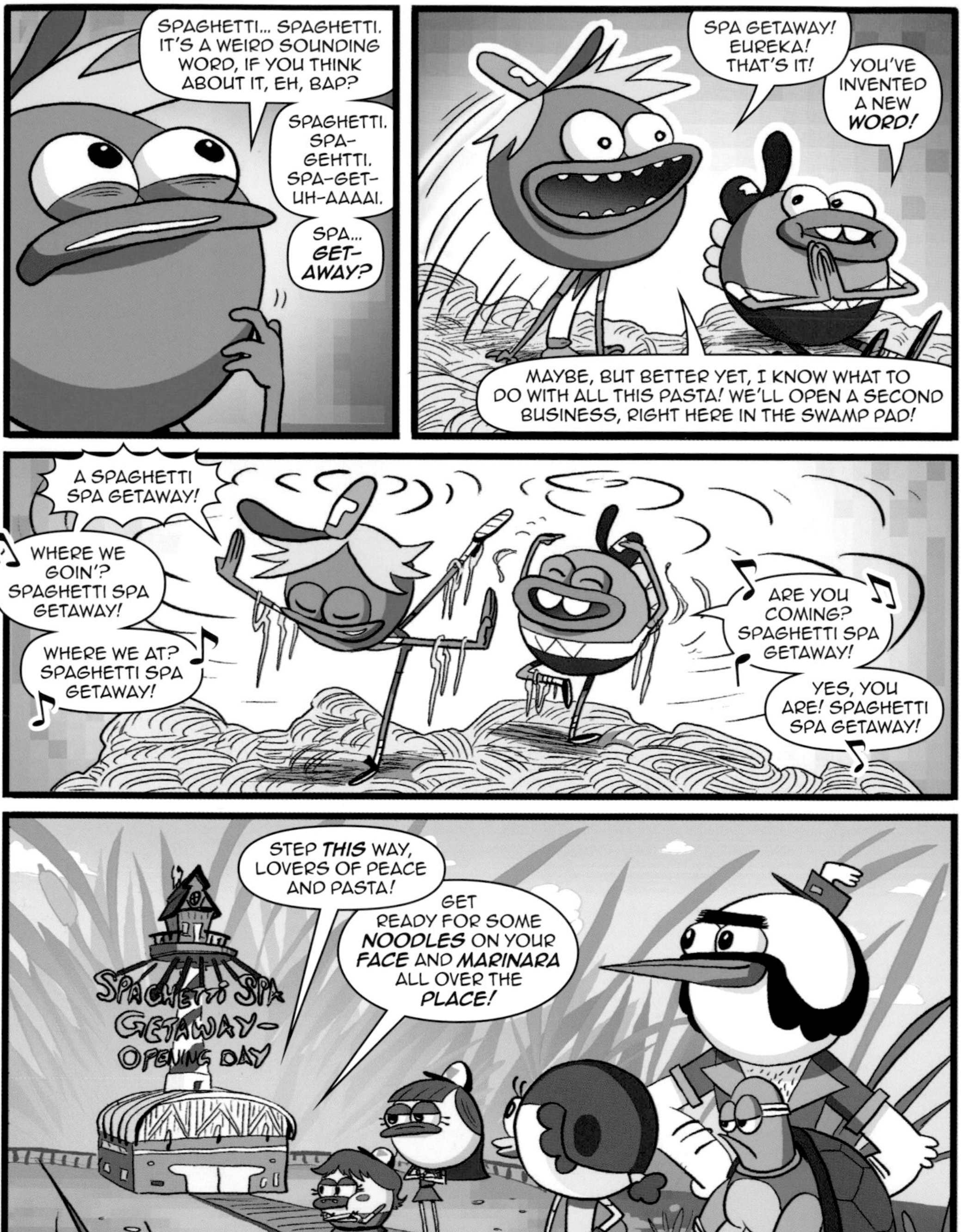
SPAGHETTI... SPAGHETTI. IT'S A WEIRD SOUNDING WORD, IF YOU THINK ABOUT IT, EH, BAP?
SPAGHETTI. SPA-GEHTTI. SPA-GET-UH-AAAAI.
SPA... GET-AWAY?
SPA GETAWAY! EUREKA! THAT'S IT!
YOU'VE INVENTED A NEW WORD!
MAYBE, BUT BETTER YET, I KNOW WHAT TO DO WITH ALL THIS PASTA! WE'LL OPEN A SECOND BUSINESS, RIGHT HERE IN THE SWAMP PAD!
A SPAGHETTI SPA GETAWAY!
WHERE WE GOIN'? SPAGHETTI SPA GETAWAY!
WHERE WE AT? SPAGHETTI SPA GETAWAY!
ARE YOU COMING? SPAGHETTI SPA GETAWAY!
YES, YOU ARE! SPAGHETTI SPA GETAWAY!
SPAGHETTI SPA GETAWAY- OPENING DAY
STEP THIS WAY, LOVERS OF PEACE AND PASTA!
GET READY FOR SOME NOODLES ON YOUR FACE AND MARINARA ALL OVER THE PLACE!

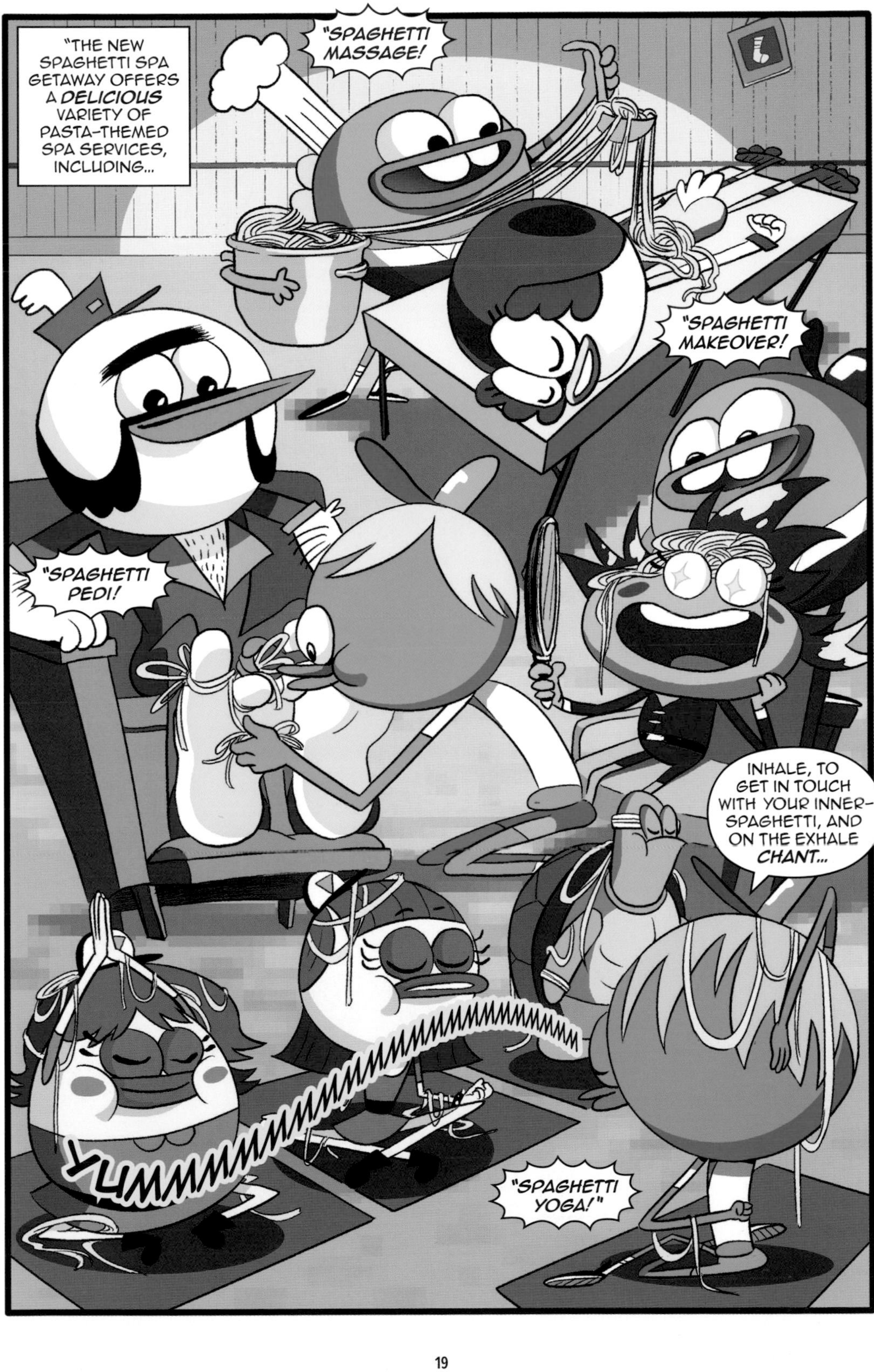
"THE NEW SPAGHETTI SPA GETAWAY OFFERS A *DELICIOUS* VARIETY OF PASTA-THEMED SPA SERVICES, INCLUDING...
"SPAGHETTI MASSAGE!
"SPAGHETTI MAKEOVER!
"SPAGHETTI PEDI!
INHALE, TO GET IN TOUCH WITH YOUR INNER-SPAGHETTI, AND ON THE EXHALE *CHANT...*
YUMMMMMMMMMMMMMMMMMMMMMMMMMMMMMMM
"SPAGHETTI YOGA!"

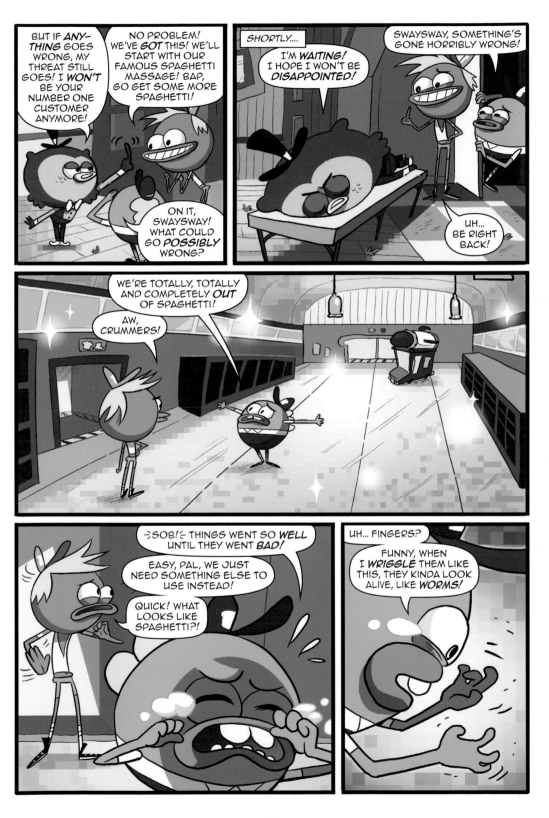

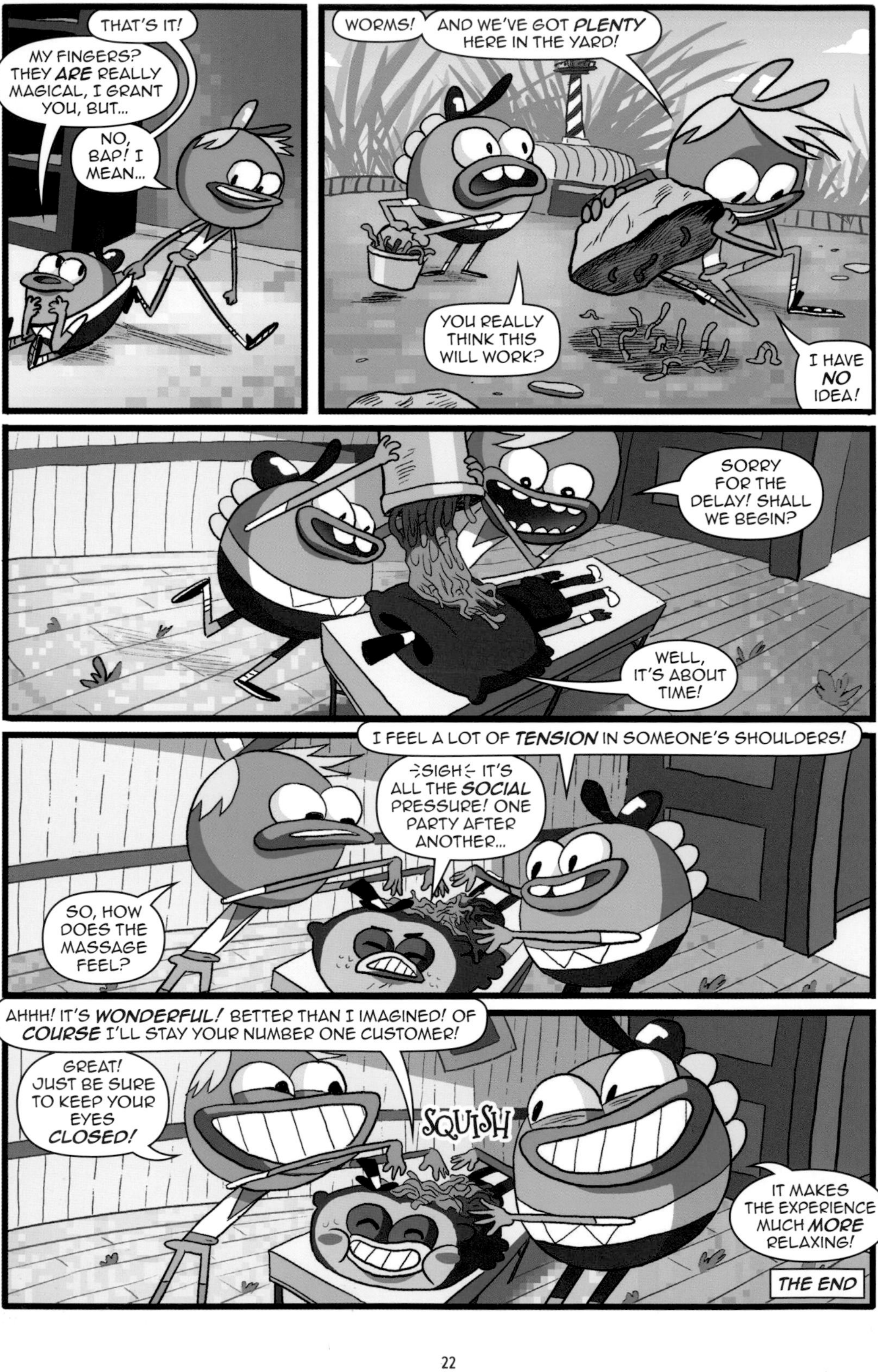

THAT'S IT!
MY FINGERS? THEY ARE REALLY MAGICAL, I GRANT YOU, BUT...
NO, BAP! I MEAN...
WORMS!
AND WE'VE GOT PLENTY HERE IN THE YARD!
YOU REALLY THINK THIS WILL WORK?
I HAVE NO IDEA!
SORRY FOR THE DELAY! SHALL WE BEGIN?
WELL, IT'S ABOUT TIME!
I FEEL A LOT OF TENSION IN SOMEONE'S SHOULDERS!
SIGH IT'S ALL THE SOCIAL PRESSURE! ONE PARTY AFTER ANOTHER...
SO, HOW DOES THE MASSAGE FEEL?
AHHH! IT'S WONDERFUL! BETTER THAN I IMAGINED! OF COURSE I'LL STAY YOUR NUMBER ONE CUSTOMER!
GREAT! JUST BE SURE TO KEEP YOUR EYES CLOSED!
SQUISH
IT MAKES THE EXPERIENCE MUCH MORE RELAXING!
THE END

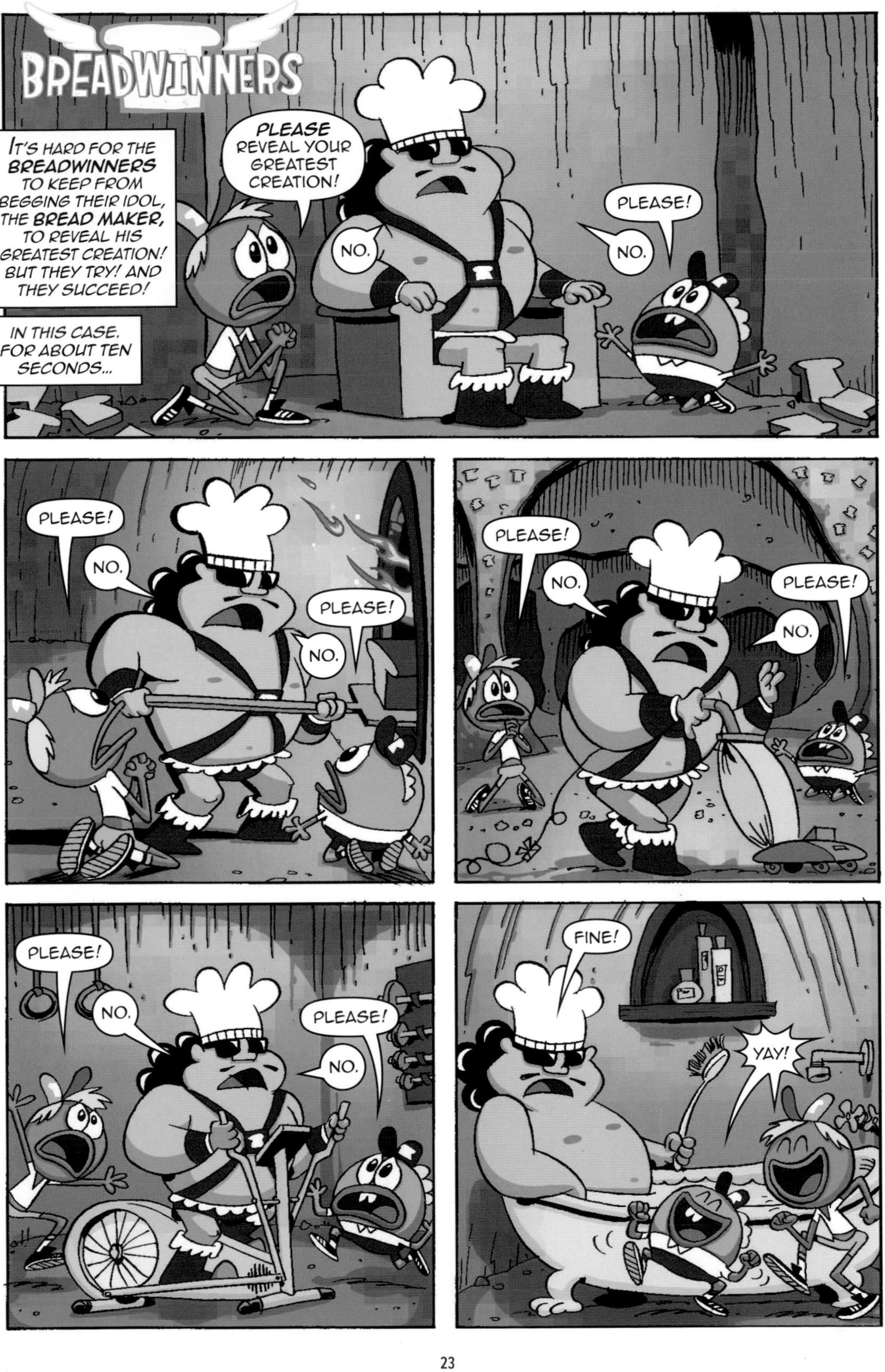
BREADWINNERS
IT'S HARD FOR THE BREADWINNERS TO KEEP FROM BEGGING THEIR IDOL, THE BREAD MAKER, TO REVEAL HIS GREATEST CREATION! BUT THEY TRY! AND THEY SUCCEED!
IN THIS CASE. FOR ABOUT TEN SECONDS...
PLEASE REVEAL YOUR GREATEST CREATION!
NO.
PLEASE!
NO.
PLEASE!
NO.
PLEASE!
NO.
PLEASE!
NO.
PLEASE!
NO.
PLEASE!
NO.
PLEASE!
NO.
FINE!
YAY!

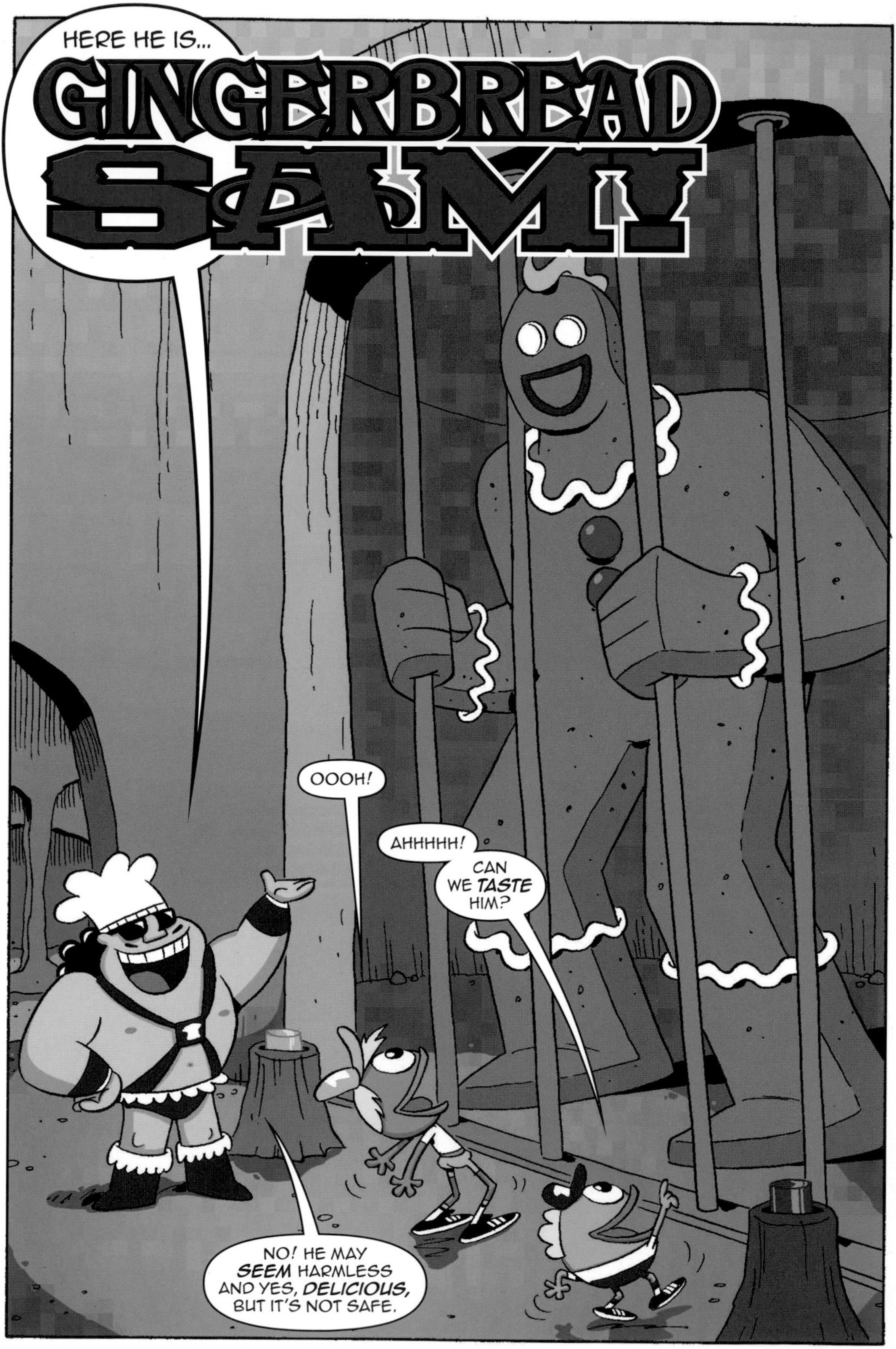
HERE HE IS...
GINGERBREAD SAMMY
OOOH!
AHHHHH!
CAN WE TASTE HIM?
NO! HE MAY SEEM HARMLESS AND YES, DELICIOUS, BUT IT'S NOT SAFE.

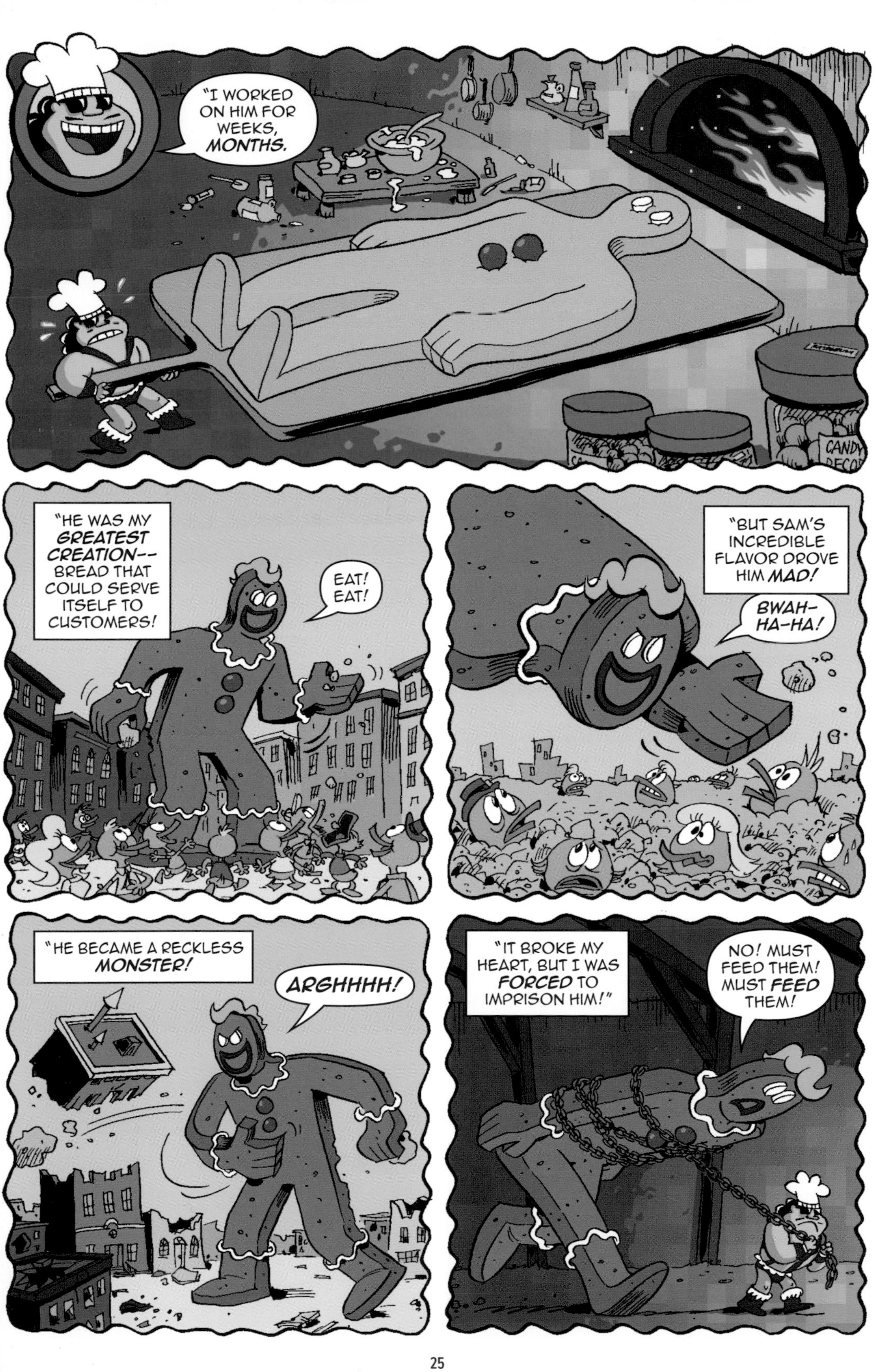
"I WORKED ON HIM FOR WEEKS, MONTHS.
"HE WAS MY GREATEST CREATION-- BREAD THAT COULD SERVE ITSELF TO CUSTOMERS!
EAT! EAT!
"BUT SAM'S INCREDIBLE FLAVOR DROVE HIM MAD!
BWAH-HA-HA!
"HE BECAME A RECKLESS MONSTER!
ARGHHHH!
"IT BROKE MY HEART, BUT I WAS FORCED TO IMPRISON HIM!"
NO! MUST FEED THEM! MUST FEED THEM!

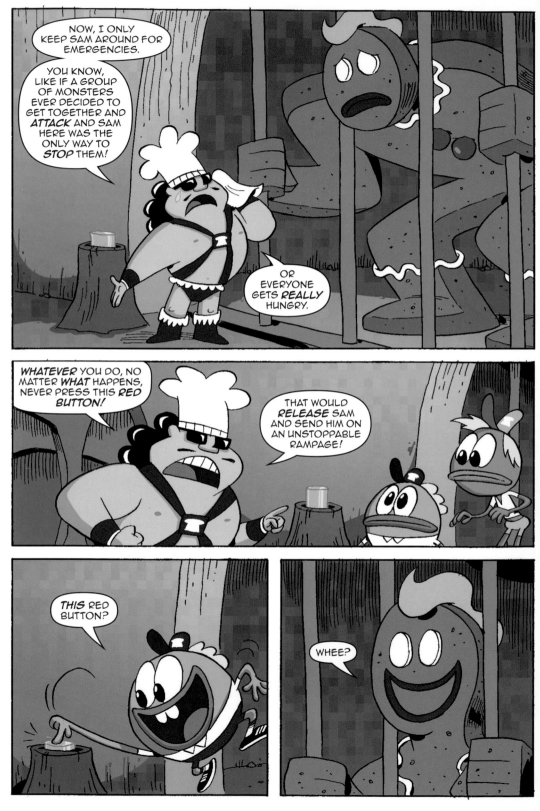

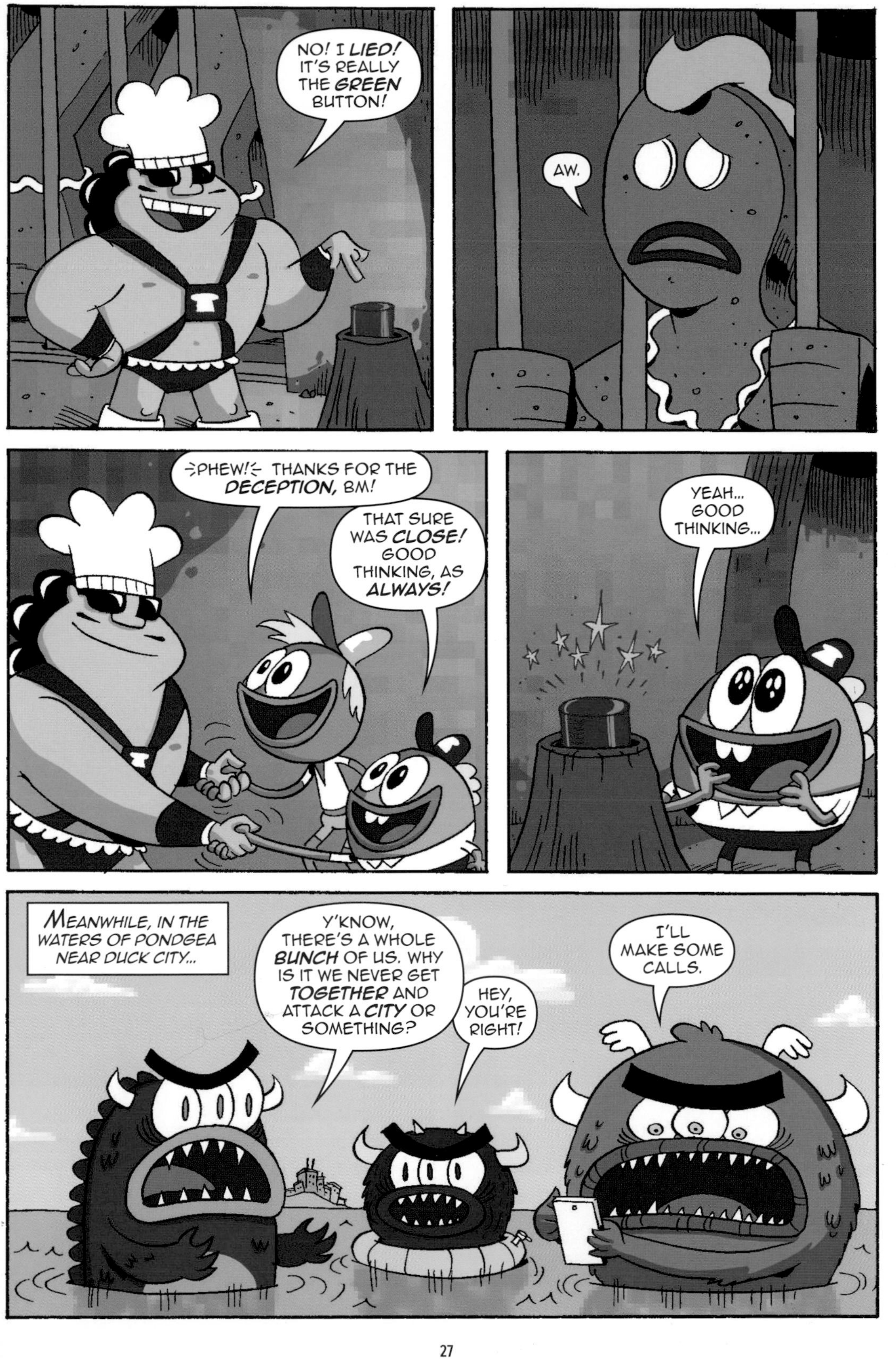
NO! I *LIED!* IT'S REALLY THE *GREEN* BUTTON!
AW.
PHEW! THANKS FOR THE *DECEPTION,* BM!
THAT SURE WAS *CLOSE!* GOOD THINKING, AS *ALWAYS!*
YEAH... GOOD THINKING...
MEANWHILE, IN THE WATERS OF PONDGEA NEAR DUCK CITY...
Y'KNOW, THERE'S A WHOLE *BUNCH* OF US. WHY IS IT WE NEVER GET *TOGETHER* AND ATTACK A *CITY* OR SOMETHING?
HEY, YOU'RE RIGHT!
I'LL MAKE SOME CALLS.

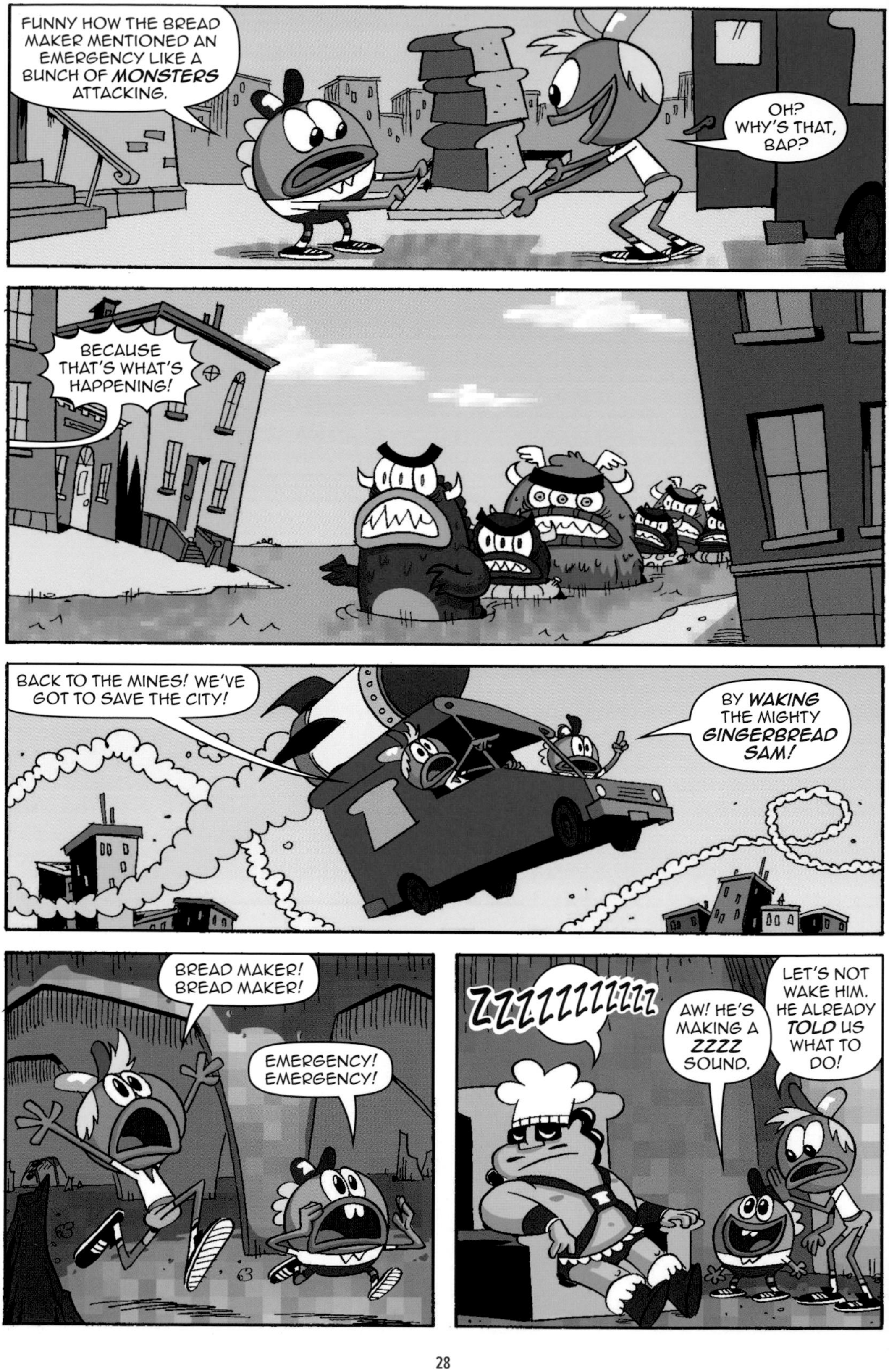
FUNNY HOW THE BREAD MAKER MENTIONED AN EMERGENCY LIKE A BUNCH OF MONSTERS ATTACKING.
OH? WHY'S THAT, BAP?
BECAUSE THAT'S WHAT'S HAPPENING!
BACK TO THE MINES! WE'VE GOT TO SAVE THE CITY!
BY WAKING THE MIGHTY GINGERBREAD SAM!
BREAD MAKER! BREAD MAKER!
EMERGENCY! EMERGENCY!
ZZZZZZZZZZZZ
AW! HE'S MAKING A ZZZZ SOUND.
LET'S NOT WAKE HIM. HE ALREADY TOLD US WHAT TO DO!

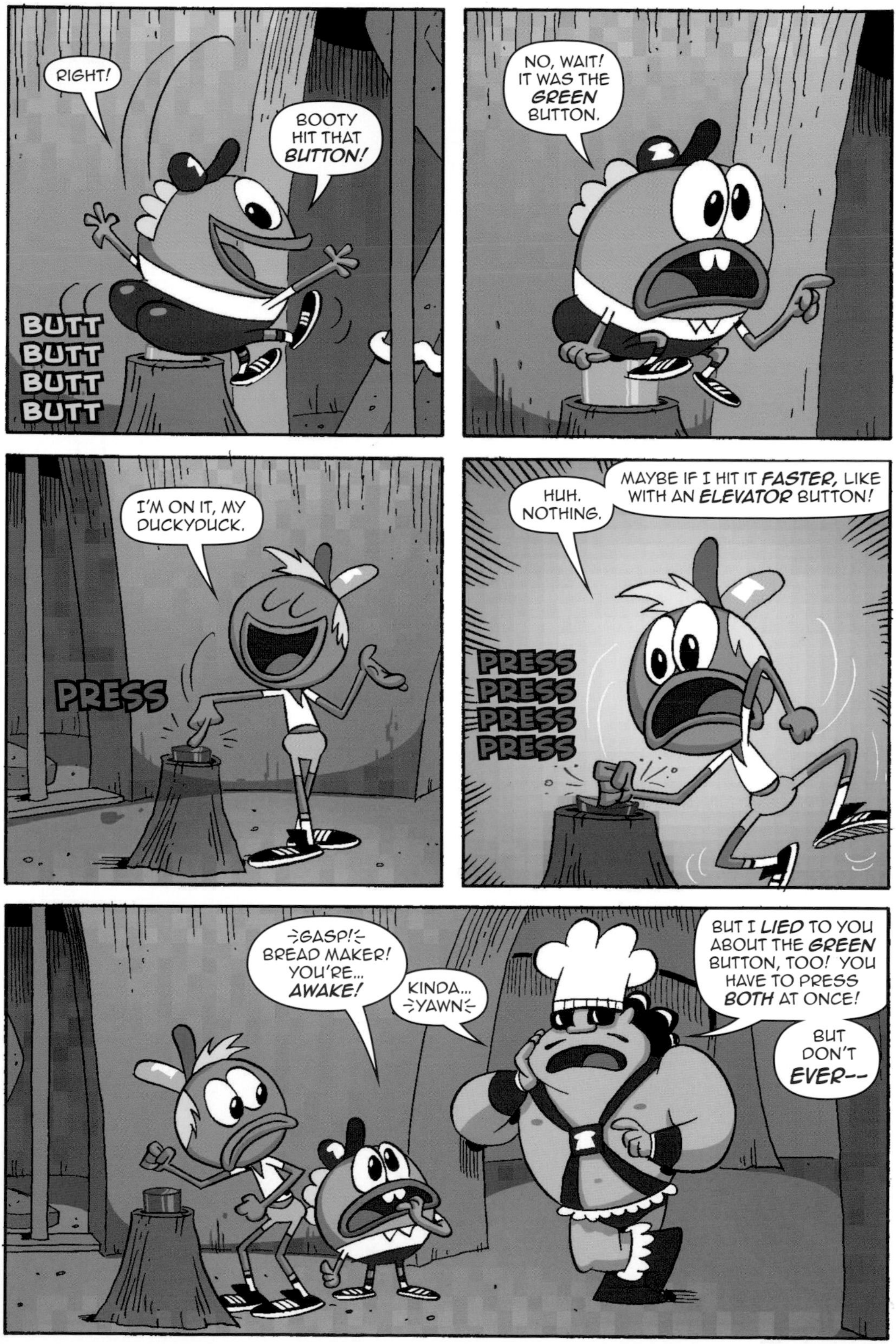
RIGHT!
BOOTY HIT THAT BUTTON!
BUTT BUTT BUTT BUTT
NO, WAIT! IT WAS THE GREEN BUTTON.
I'M ON IT, MY DUCKYDUCK.
PRESS
HUH. NOTHING.
MAYBE IF I HIT IT FASTER, LIKE WITH AN ELEVATOR BUTTON!
PRESS PRESS PRESS PRESS
GASP! BREAD MAKER! YOU'RE... AWAKE!
KINDA... YAWN
BUT I LIED TO YOU ABOUT THE GREEN BUTTON, TOO! YOU HAVE TO PRESS BOTH AT ONCE!
BUT DON'T EVER--

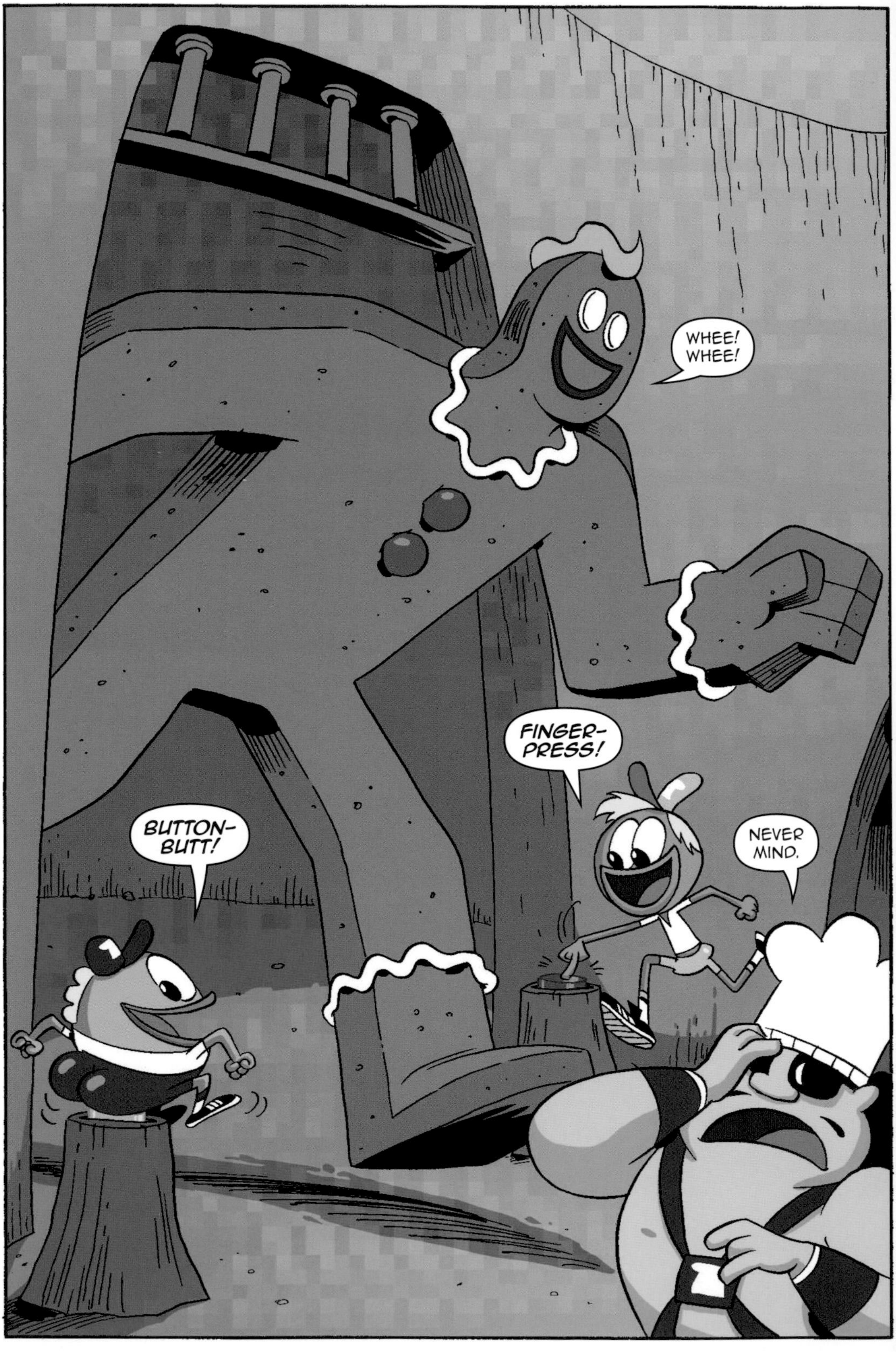
WHEE! WHEE!
FINGER-PRESS!
BUTTON-BUTT!
NEVER MIND.

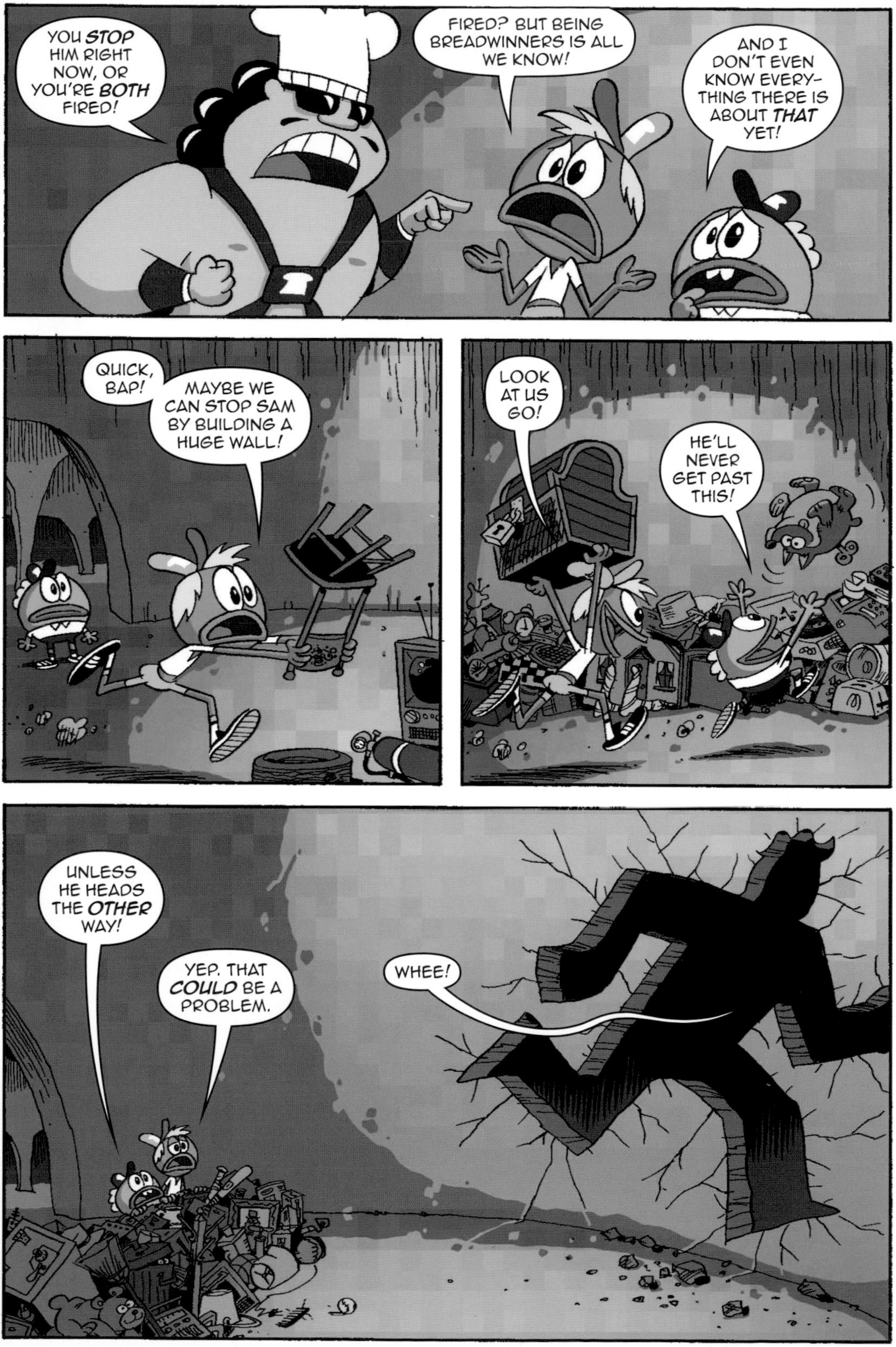
YOU STOP HIM RIGHT NOW, OR YOU'RE BOTH FIRED!
FIRED? BUT BEING BREADWINNERS IS ALL WE KNOW!
AND I DON'T EVEN KNOW EVERY-THING THERE IS ABOUT THAT YET!
QUICK, BAP!
MAYBE WE CAN STOP SAM BY BUILDING A HUGE WALL!
LOOK AT US GO!
HE'LL NEVER GET PAST THIS!
UNLESS HE HEADS THE OTHER WAY!
YEP. THAT COULD BE A PROBLEM.
WHEE!

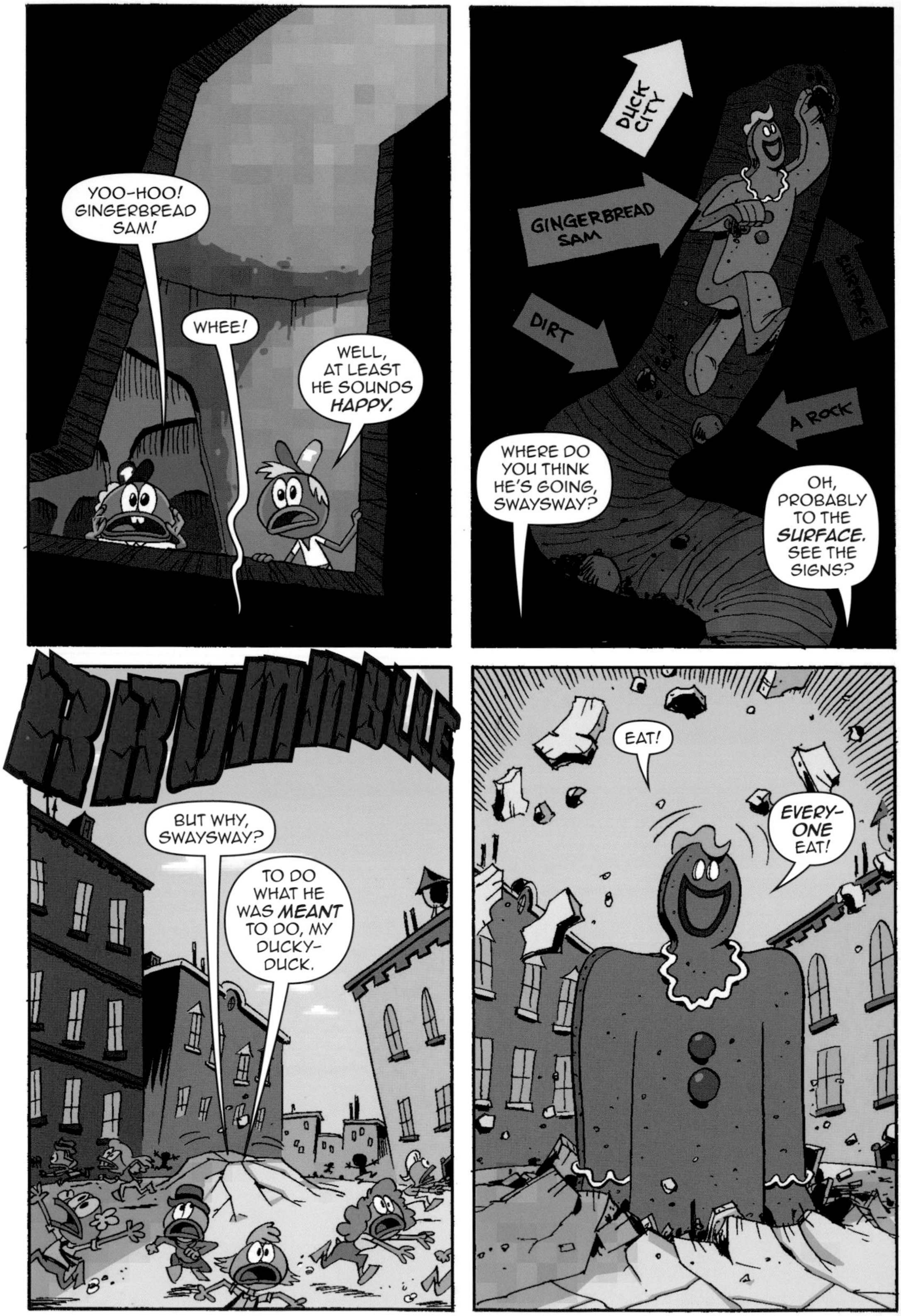
YOO-HOO! GINGERBREAD SAM!
WHEE!
WELL, AT LEAST HE SOUNDS *HAPPY.*
DUCK CITY
GINGERBREAD SAM
DIRT
A ROCK
WHERE DO YOU THINK HE'S GOING, SWAYSWAY?
OH, PROBABLY TO THE *SURFACE.* SEE THE SIGNS?
BUT WHY, SWAYSWAY?
TO DO WHAT HE WAS *MEANT* TO DO, MY DUCKY-DUCK.
EAT!
EVERY-ONE EAT!

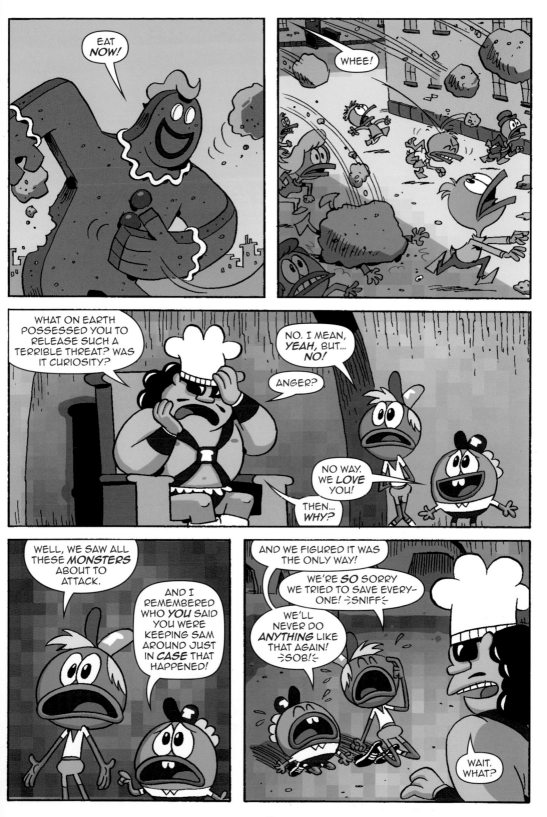

EAT *NOW!*

WHEE!

WHAT ON EARTH POSSESSED YOU TO RELEASE SUCH A TERRIBLE THREAT? WAS IT CURIOSITY?

NO. I MEAN, *YEAH,* BUT... *NO!*

ANGER?

NO WAY. WE *LOVE* YOU!

THEN... *WHY?*

WELL, WE SAW ALL THESE *MONSTERS* ABOUT TO ATTACK.

AND I REMEMBERED WHO *YOU* SAID YOU WERE KEEPING SAM AROUND JUST IN *CASE* THAT HAPPENED!

AND WE FIGURED IT WAS THE ONLY WAY!

WE'RE *SO* SORRY WE TRIED TO SAVE EVERY-ONE! ÷SNIFF÷

WE'LL NEVER DO *ANYTHING* LIKE THAT AGAIN! ÷SOB!÷

WAIT. WHAT?

33

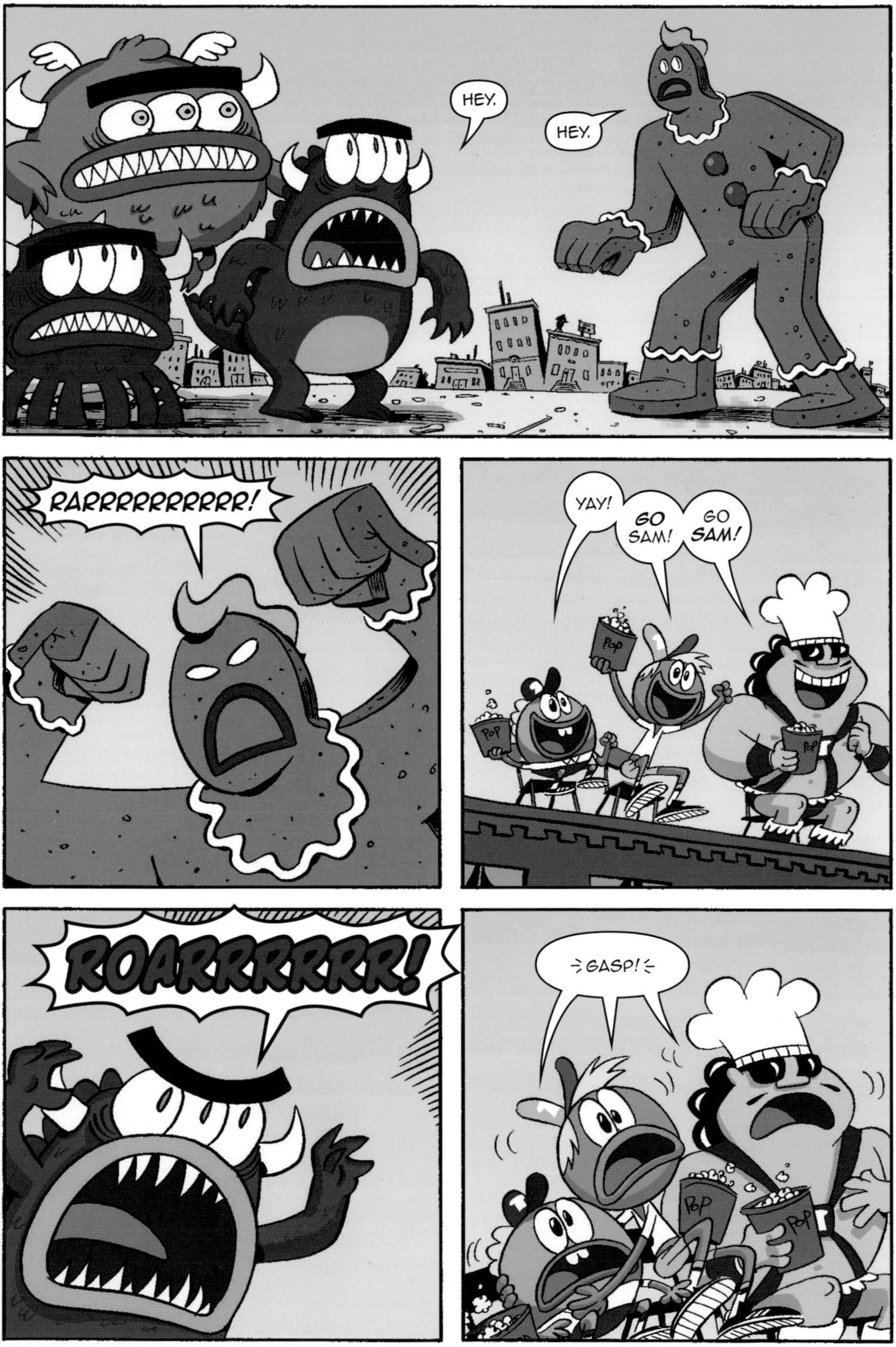
HEY.
HEY.
RARRRRRRRRRR!
YAY!
GO SAM!
GO SAM!
ROARRRRRRR!
GASP!

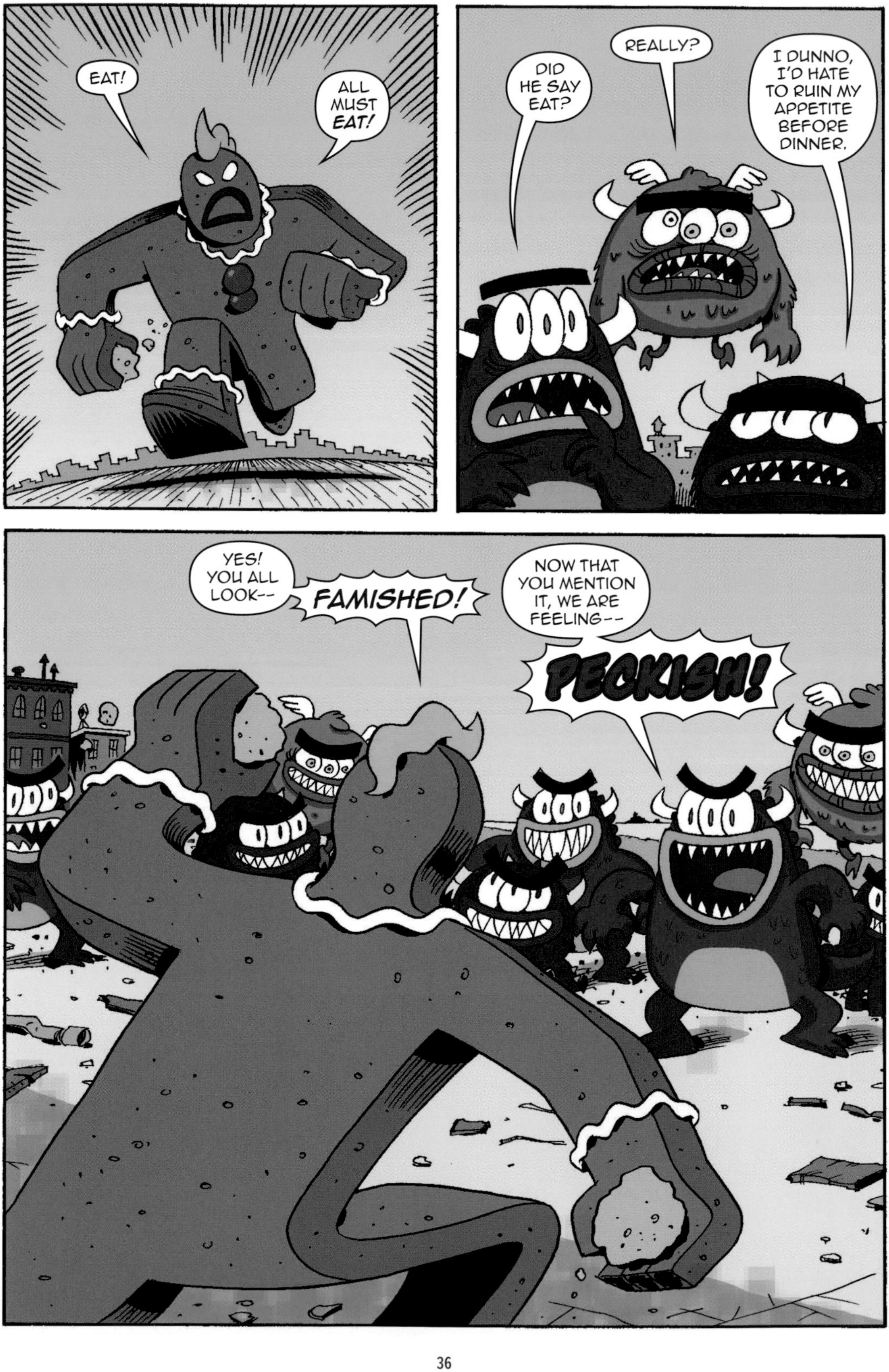
EAT!
ALL MUST EAT!
DID HE SAY EAT?
REALLY?
I DUNNO, I'D HATE TO RUIN MY APPETITE BEFORE DINNER.
YES! YOU ALL LOOK--
FAMISHED!
NOW THAT YOU MENTION IT, WE ARE FEELING--
PECKISH!

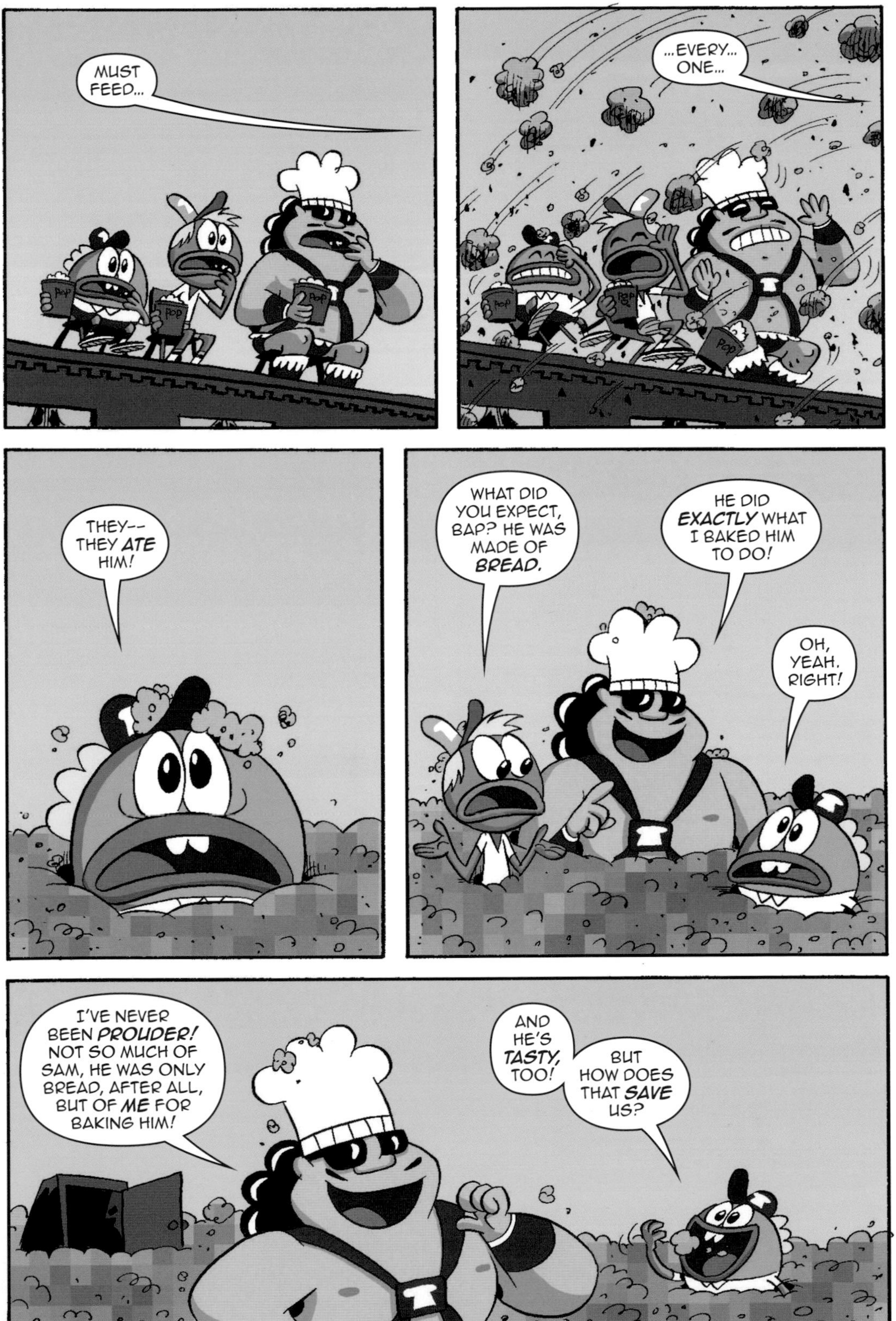
MUST FEED...
...EVERY... ONE...
THEY-- THEY *ATE* HIM!
WHAT DID YOU EXPECT, BAP? HE WAS MADE OF *BREAD.*
HE DID *EXACTLY* WHAT I BAKED HIM TO DO!
OH, YEAH. RIGHT!
I'VE NEVER BEEN *PROUDER!* NOT SO MUCH OF SAM, HE WAS ONLY BREAD, AFTER ALL, BUT OF *ME* FOR BAKING HIM!
AND HE'S *TASTY,* TOO!
BUT HOW DOES THAT *SAVE* US?

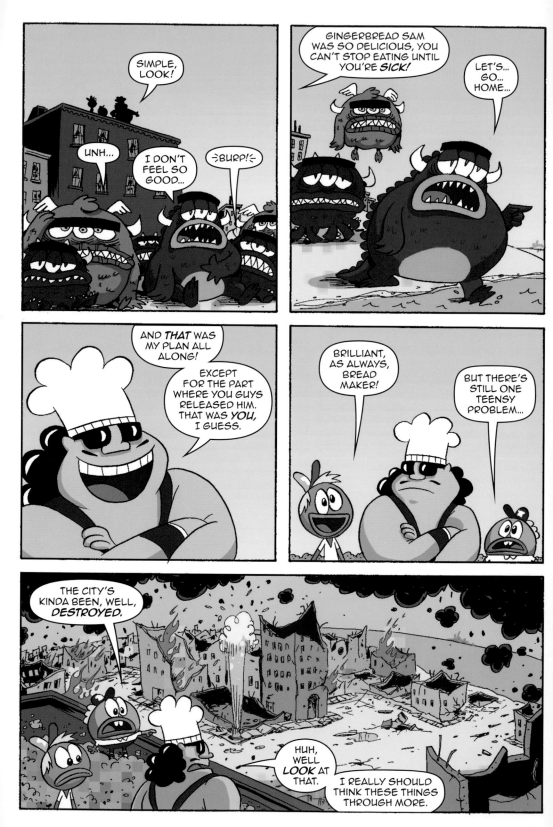

WATCH OUT FOR PAPERCUTZ

Welcome to the slightly-toasted, salt-free second **BREADWINNERS** graphic novel from Papercutz—those somewhat doughy comic-makers dedicated to publishing great graphic novels for all ages. I'm Jim Salicrup, the Silvercup-Bread-loving Editor-in-Chief, and I'm here to share with you all our plans for the future (world domination?) and take you behind the scenes here at Papercutz.

We've got really great news and some somewhat sad news. Just so you don't get anxious, we'll start with the sad news first. This edition of **BREADWINNERS** is the last one Papercutz will be publishing. Hey, don't worry—it's not the end of the world! Especially when you hear our good news...

Coming soon to the bookseller near you will be an all-new Nickelodeon graphic novel series entitled **NICKELODEON PANDEMONIUM!** What's that? You've never heard of that show? That's because it isn't a show, it's an ongoing graphic novel series that will feature comics starring the very best new Nickelodeon cartoon stars—such as Sanjay and Craig, Harvey Peaks, Pig Goat Banana Cricket, and—you guessed it!—Breadwinners!

They say variety is the spice of life, so what could be more fun than a graphic novel featuring lots of your favorite Nickelodeon characters? Well, you might argue that the monthly **NICKELODEON MAGAZINE** might be more fun, but the graphic novel will contain **MORE** pages than an issue of the magazine, so you'll be getting **MORE** in the graphic novel series!

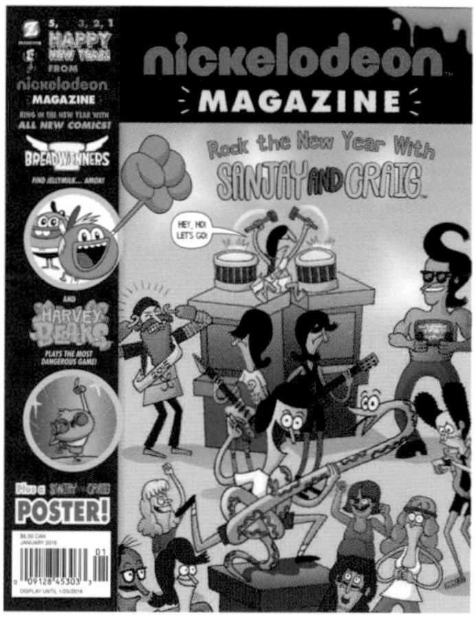
nickelodeon
MAGAZINE
Rock the New Year With
SANJAY AND CRAIG
HEY, HO! LET'S GO!
BREADWINNERS
HARVEY BEAKS
POSTER!

Speaking of **NICKELODEON MAGAZINE**, look for Buhdeuce and SwaySway to keep popping up in those pages as well. Let's face it—we love those guys and can't get enough of them. So after you've seen every **BREADWINNERS** cartoon on Nickelodeon, don't forget that Papercutz is **THE** place now to get all-new stories starring your favorite bread-delivering ducks!

Thanks,

Jim

STAY IN TOUCH!

EMAIL:	salicrup@papercutz.com
WEB:	papercutz.com
TWITTER:	@papercutzgn
FACEBOOK:	PAPERCUTZGRAPHICNOVELS
FANMAIL:	Papercutz, 160 Broadway, Suite 700, East Wing, New York, NY 10038

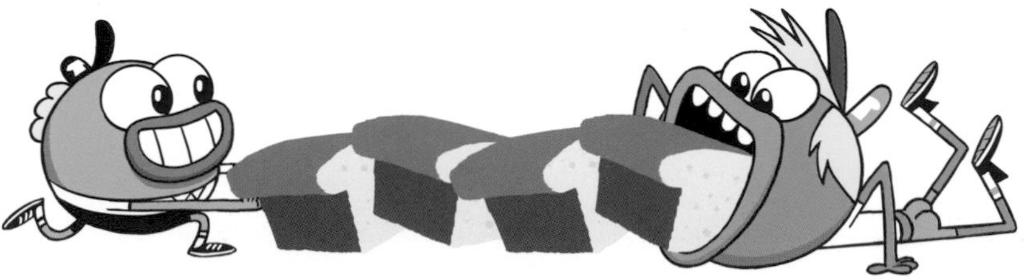

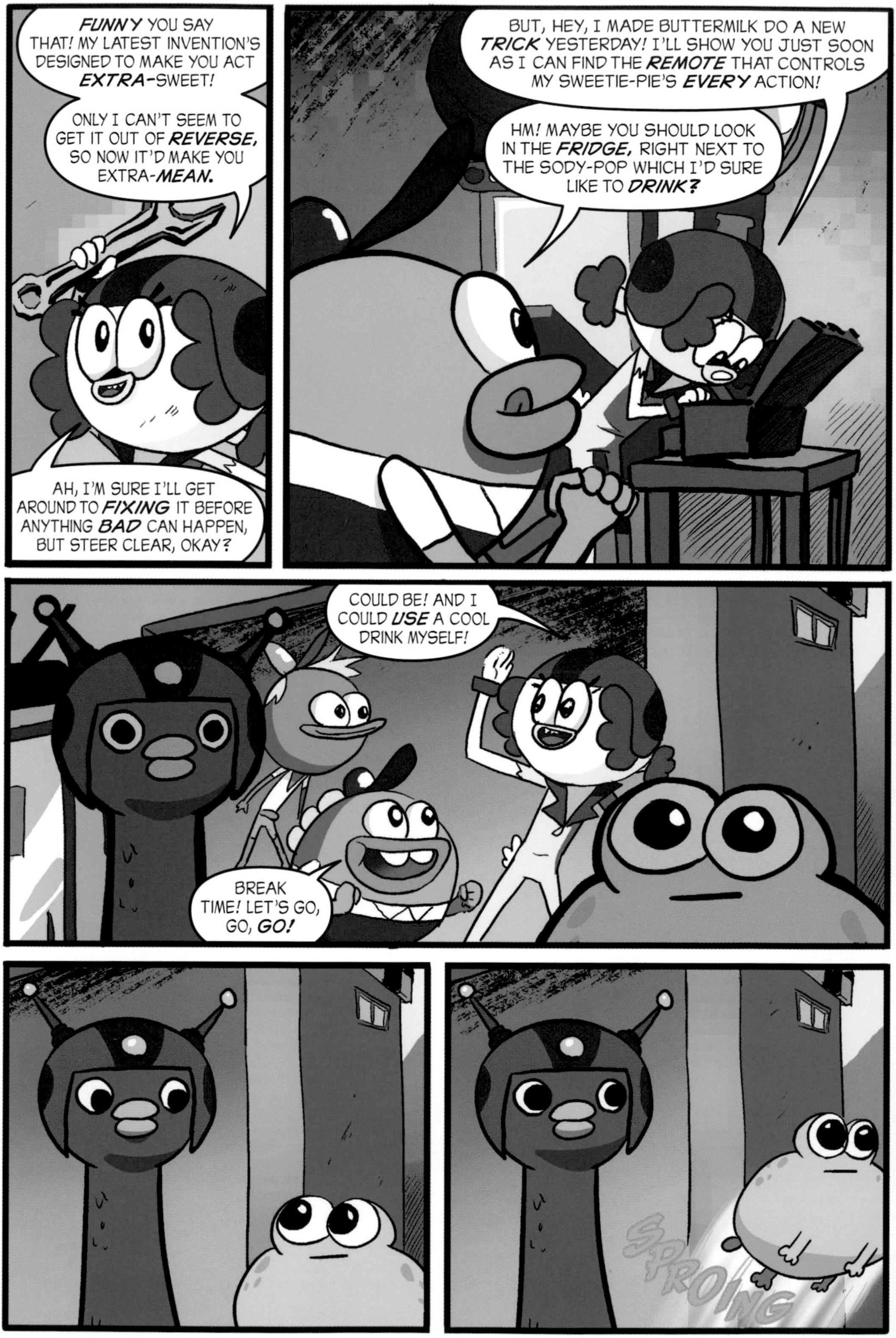
FUNNY YOU SAY THAT! MY LATEST INVENTION'S DESIGNED TO MAKE YOU ACT EXTRA-SWEET!
ONLY I CAN'T SEEM TO GET IT OUT OF REVERSE, SO NOW IT'D MAKE YOU EXTRA-MEAN.
AH, I'M SURE I'LL GET AROUND TO FIXING IT BEFORE ANYTHING BAD CAN HAPPEN, BUT STEER CLEAR, OKAY?
BUT, HEY, I MADE BUTTERMILK DO A NEW TRICK YESTERDAY! I'LL SHOW YOU JUST SOON AS I CAN FIND THE REMOTE THAT CONTROLS MY SWEETIE-PIE'S EVERY ACTION!
HM! MAYBE YOU SHOULD LOOK IN THE FRIDGE, RIGHT NEXT TO THE SODY-POP WHICH I'D SURE LIKE TO DRINK?
COULD BE! AND I COULD USE A COOL DRINK MYSELF!
BREAK TIME! LET'S GO, GO, GO!
SPROING

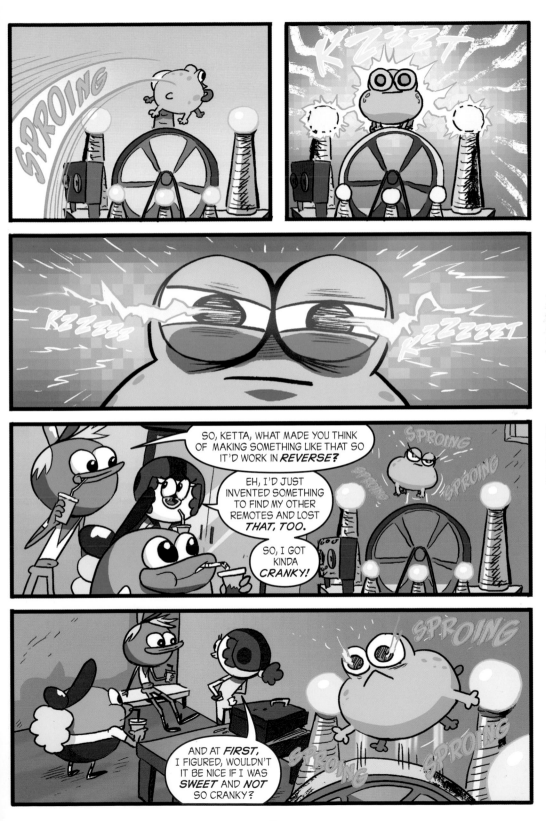

44

45

48

49

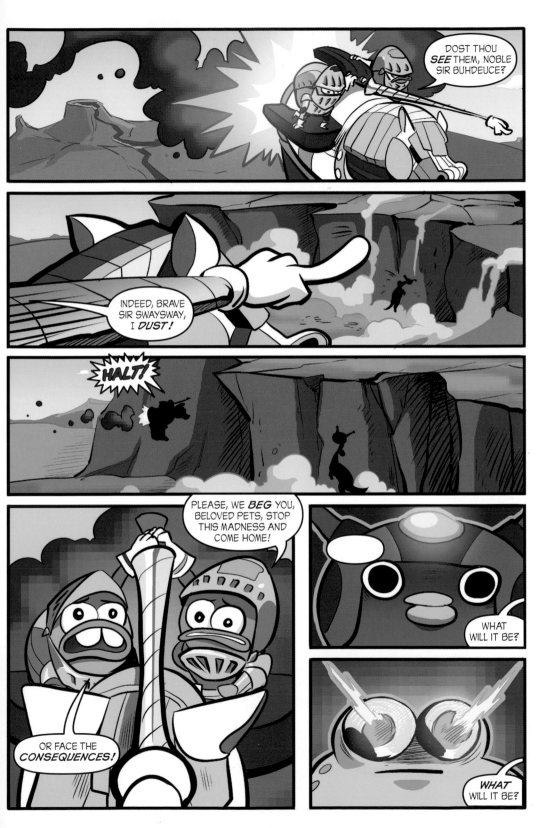

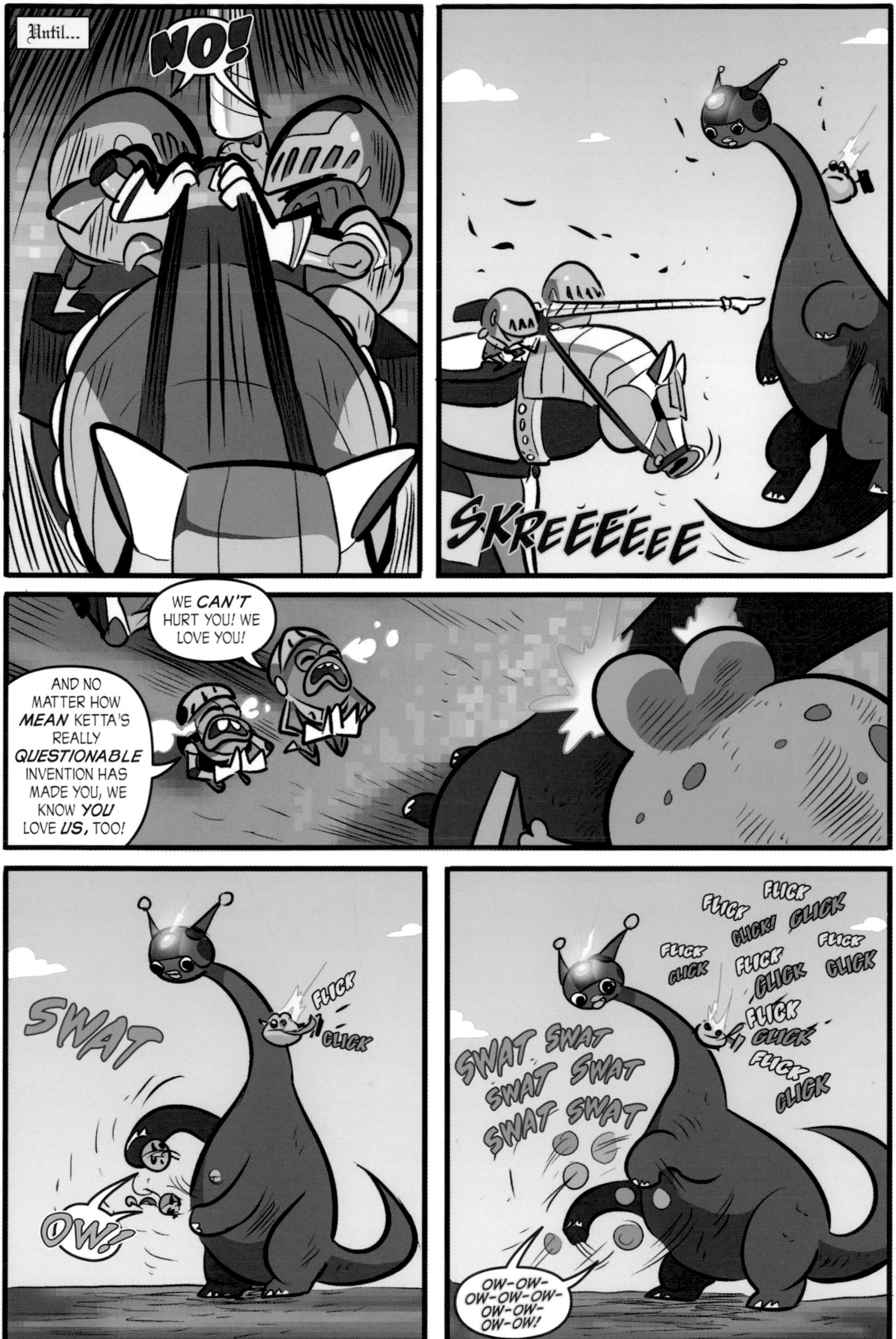

Until...
NO!
SKREEEEEEE
WE CAN'T HURT YOU! WE LOVE YOU!
AND NO MATTER HOW MEAN KETTA'S REALLY QUESTIONABLE INVENTION HAS MADE YOU, WE KNOW YOU LOVE US, TOO!
SWAT
FLICK
CLICK
OW!
FLICK
FLICK
CLICK!
CLICK
FLICK
CLICK
FLICK
CLICK
FLICK
CLICK
SWAT SWAT
SWAT SWAT
SWAT SWAT
FLICK
CLICK
FLICK
CLICK
OW-OW-OW-OW-OW-OW-OW-OW-OW!